Nick's heart pumped sheer adrenaline throughout his body as he quickly pulled his gun. He stared in the direction that the bullet had come from but saw nobody.

Sarah was still as a statue beneath him. "Are you okay?" he asked softly.

"I'm fine," she replied, but he could feel the frantic beat of her heart against his.

"What the hell was that all about?" he asked.

"It's possible somebody just warned us off our investigation," she replied.

"Did it work? Do you want to be reassigned?"

"Heck no," she replied, her eyes lit with blue fire. "This just makes me more determined than ever to go forward."

He gazed at her for a long moment. That bullet aimed at them would have shaken up the most seasoned professional, but she appeared to have taken it in stride. Either she had a good poker face or she was utterly fearless.

WETLANDS INVESTIGATION

New York Times Bestselling Author

CARLA CASSIDY

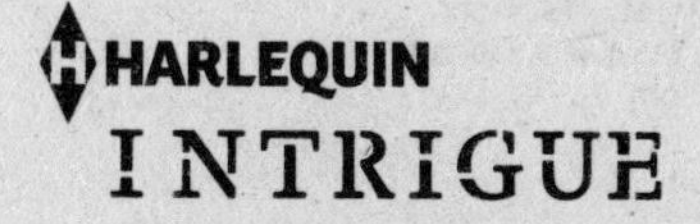

HARLEQUIN® INTRIGUE™

Recycling programs for this product may not exist in your area.

ISBN-13: 978-1-335-59145-6

Wetlands Investigation

For questions and comments about the quality of this book, please contact us at CustomerService@Harlequin.com.

Harlequin Enterprises ULC
22 Adelaide St. West, 41st Floor
Toronto, Ontario M5H 4E3, Canada
www.Harlequin.com

Printed in U.S.A.

Carla Cassidy is an award-winning, *New York Times* bestselling author who has written over 170 books, including 150 for Harlequin. She has won the Centennial Award from Romance Writers of America. Most recently she won the 2019 Write Touch Readers' Award for her Harlequin Intrigue title *Desperate Strangers*. Carla believes the only thing better than curling up with a good book is sitting down at the computer with a good story to write.

Books by Carla Cassidy

Harlequin Intrigue

The Swamp Slayings

Unsolved Bayou Murder
Monster in the Marsh
Wetlands Investigation

Kings of Coyote Creek

Closing in on the Cowboy
Revenge on the Ranch
Gunsmoke in the Grassland

Desperate Strangers
Desperate Intentions
Desperate Measures
Stalked in the Night
Stalker in the Shadows

Visit the Author Profile page at Harlequin.com.

CAST OF CHARACTERS

Nick Cain—Hired to solve the monster murders, he catches himself falling for the officer assigned to work with him.

Sarah Beauregard—Frustrated with her work, she finds Nick a very hot distraction.

Gator Broussard—What exactly does the old man know about the swamp monster?

Ed Martin—Why did the businessman always show up when a victim was found?

James Noman—A mysterious man who lives in the swamp—was he committing the heinous murders?

Deputy Ryan Staub—Is he really a good lawman or a cold-blooded killer?

Chapter One

Private investigator Nick Cain drove slowly down the main street of the small town of Black Bayou, Louisiana. It was his first opportunity getting a look at the place where he'd be living and working for at least the next three months or longer if necessary.

His first impression was that the buildings all looked a bit old and tired. However, in the distance the swamp that nearly surrounded the town appeared to breathe with life and color. And it was in the swamp he believed he would do much of his investigation. At the very thought of going into the marshland, a wave of nervous energy tightened his stomach muscles.

He'd been hired by Chief of Police Thomas Gravois to assist in the investigation of four murdered woman. Apparently, a serial murderer was at play in the small town. He would work as an independent contractor and not as a member of the official law enforcement team.

Before he checked in with Chief Gravois, he needed

to find the place he'd rented for his time here. It was Gravois who had turned him on to the room for rent in Irene Tompkin's home. Irene was a widow who rented out rooms in her house for extra money.

Once he turned on to Cypress Street, he looked for the correct address. He found it and pulled into the driveway. The widow Tompkin's home was a nice, large two-story painted beige with brown shutters and trim. An expansive wraparound porch held wicker furniture and a swing that invited a person to sit and enjoy. The neighborhood was nice with well-kept lawns and older homes.

He decided to introduce himself first before pulling out all his luggage so he got out of the car, walked up to the front door and knocked. The early September sun was hot on his back as he waited for somebody to answer.

A diminutive woman with a shock of white hair and bright blue eyes opened the door and her wrinkled face wreathed with a friendly smile. "Even though you're a very handsome young man, I'm sorry but I'm not buying anything today," she said.

"That's good because I'm not selling anything. My name is Nick..."

"Oh, Mr. Cain," she replied before he had even fully introduced himself. "I've been expecting you." She grabbed his hand and tugged him over the threshold. "I'm so glad you're here. It's such an honor for you to stay in my home and the town needs you desperately. Let me show you the room where you'll be staying." She continued to pull him toward the large staircase. "How was your trip here?"

"It was fine," he replied, and gently pulled his hand from hers as he followed her up to the second floor.

"Good…good. I baked some cookies earlier. I thought you might want a little snack before you get to your detective work." They reached the top of the stairs and walked down a short hall, and then she opened a door and gestured him to follow her inside.

The bedroom sported a king-size bed, a dresser and an en suite bathroom. The beige walls complemented the cool mint-green color scheme. There was also a small table with two chairs in front of the large window that looked out on the street and a door that led to an old iron fire escape staircase to the ground.

"Is this okay for your needs?" She turned to look at him, her blue eyes filled with obvious apprehension.

He smiled at her. "This is absolutely perfect." It was actually far better than he'd expected. His main requirement was that the place be clean, and this space screamed and smelled of cleanliness.

"Oh good, I'm so glad. Well, I'll just leave you to get settled in and then we can have a little chat?"

"Of course," he replied.

She scurried out of the room and he followed after her. At the foot of the stairs, she beelined into another area of the house and he went outside to retrieve his luggage.

Within thirty minutes he was unpacked. He went back downstairs and stood in the entry. “Mrs. Tompkin,” he hollered.

She appeared in one of the doorways and offered him another bright smile. “Come,” she said. “I’ve got some cookies for you and we can have a little chitchat about house rules and such.”

The kitchen was large and airy with windows across one wall and a wooden table that sat six. She ushered him into one of the chairs. In the center of the table was a platter of what appeared to be chocolate chip cookies.

“Would you like a cup of coffee?” she asked.

“That sounds nice,” he replied.

“It’s so easy now to make a cup of coffee with this newfangled coffee maker,” she said as she popped a pod into the machine. She then reached on her tippytoes and pulled a saucer from one of the cabinets and carried it over to the table.

“You have a very nice place here,” Nick said.

She beamed at him as she placed three cookies on the saucer and then set it before him. “Thank you. Me and my husband, Henry, God rest his soul, were very happy here for a lot of years. He passed five years ago from colon cancer.”

“I’m so sorry for your loss,” he replied.

“It’s okay now. I know he’s up in heaven holding a spot for me. And that reminds me, there's no Mrs. Tompkin here. Everyone just calls me Nene."

"Then Nene it will be," he replied.

"I just thought we needed to chat about how things go around here. I have one other boarder. His name is Ralph Summerset. He's a nice man who mostly stays to himself. He's retired from the army and now works part-time at the post office. Cream or sugar?" she asked as she set the cup of coffee in front of him.

"Black is just fine," he replied.

She sat on the chair opposite him and smiled at him once again. Nick would guess her to be in her late seventies or early eighties, but she gave off much younger vibes and energy.

"Anyway, I provide breakfast anytime between six and eight in the mornings and then I cook a nice meal at around five thirty each evening. If you're here, you can eat, but if you aren't here, I don't provide around-the-clock services."

"Understandable," he replied. Even though he wasn't a bit hungry at the moment, he bit into one of the cookies.

"I usually require my guests to be home by ten or so, but I'm making an exception for you." She reached into the pocket of the blue housedress she wore and pulled out a key. "I know with your line of work, your hours are going to be crazy, so take this and then you can come and go as you please. Just make sure when you come in you lock up the door behind you."

"Thank you, I appreciate that." He took the key from her and then finished the cookie and took a sip of his coffee. He was eager to get to the police station and find out just what he was dealing with, but he also knew it was important to build relationships with the locals. And that started here with Nene.

He picked up the second cookie. "These are really delicious," he said, making her beam a smile at him once again.

"I enjoy baking, so I hope you like sweets," she said.

"I definitely have a sweet tooth," he replied. "And I'm sorry, but two cookies are enough for me right now." He took another drink of his coffee.

"I hope you're good at detecting things because these murders that are taking place are frightening and something needs to be done to get the Honey Island Swamp Monster murderer behind bars."

"Honey Island Swamp Monster?" He gazed at her curiously, having not heard the term before.

"That's what everyone is calling the murderer," she replied.

"And who or what is the Honey Island Swamp Monster?"

She leaned forward in her chair, her eyes sparkling like those of a mischievous child. "Legend has it that he was an abandoned child raised by alligators. He's supposed to be over seven feet tall and weighs about four hundred pounds. He has long dirty gray hair and golden eyes, and he stinks to high heaven."

Nick looked at her in disbelief. "Surely nobody really believes that's what killed those women."

Nene leaned back in her chair and released a titter of laughter. "Of course not." The merriment left her face as she frowned at him. "The sad part is now you got town people thinking somebody from the swamp is responsible and the swamp people think somebody from town is responsible and our chief of police seems to be clueless about all of it."

She reached across the table and grabbed one of Nick's hands. "All that really matters is that there's somebody out there killing these poor young women and the rumors are the killings are horribly savage. I really hope you can help us, Mr. Cain." She released his hand.

"Please, make it Nick," he replied as he tried to digest everything she'd just told him. He'd learned over the years not to discount any piece of information he got about a particular crime. Even rumors and gossip had a place in a criminal investigation.

She smiled at him again. "Then Nick it is," she said. "Anyway, Nick, I read a lot of romance books and you look like the handsome stranger who comes to town and not only saves the day but also finds his one true love. Do you have a one true love, Nick? Is there somebody waiting for you back home?"

"No, I'm pretty much married to my job."

"Well, that's a darned shame," she replied. "Now don't make me stop believing in my romances."

"I'm sorry, but I'm definitely no romance hero," he replied. His ex-wife would certainly agree with his assessment of himself. Three years ago, Amy had divorced him because he wasn't her hero. At that time, he'd permanently written love out of his life.

His work was what he could depend on and thinking of that, he rose to his feet and grabbed the house key from the table. "If we're finished here, I really need to get to the police station and get to work."

"Of course, I didn't mean to hold you up as long as I have." She got out of her chair and walked with him to the front door. "I hope to see you for dinner, but I'll understand if you can't make it. I know you have important work to do so I won't delay you any longer."

They said their goodbyes and Nick got back in his car to head to the police station. As he drove toward Main Street, he thought about Nene and the conversation he'd just had with her.

His impression of his landlady was that she was a sweet older woman who was more than a bit lonely. He had a feeling if he would have continued to sit at the table, she would have been perfectly satisfied talking to him for the rest of the afternoon.

With his living space sorted out he could now focus on the reason he was here. When he'd seen the ad in the paper looking for help in solving a series of murders, he had definitely been intrigued.

He'd spent years working as a homicide detective in the New Orleans Police Department. He'd won plenty of accolades and awards for his work and he'd labored hard on putting away as many murderers as possible. However, two years ago he'd decided to quit the department and open his own private investigation business, but that certainly hadn't meant he was done with killers.

When he'd reached out to Thomas Gravois, the man had told him about the four young women from the swamp who had been brutally murdered by the same killer, but he hadn't said anything about fighting between the swamp people and town people. In fact, Nene had given him more information about the crimes than Gravois had.

Still, that didn't matter. Gravois had hired him over a phone call after seeing all of Nick's credentials. Nick was now more intrigued than ever to get a look at the murder books and see where the investigations had gone so far and what kind of "monster" he was dealing with.

He didn't know if his fresh eyes and skills could solve these murders, but he'd give his all to see that four murdered women got the justice they deserved.

SARAH BEAUREGARD SAT at the dispatch/reception desk in the police office lobby and drummed her fingernails on the top as nervous energy bubbled around in the pit of her tummy.

She'd been working for the police department since she was twenty-one years old and for the past twelve years Chief Gravois had kept her either on desk duty or parked just off Main Street to hand out speeding tickets.

Over those years she'd begged him to allow her to work on any of the cases that had come up, but he'd refused. She had just turned twenty-one when her parents had been killed in a head-on collision with a drunk driver.

She'd been reeling with grief and loss and Gravois, who had been close friends with her father, had taken her under his wing and hired her on as a police officer. However, his protectiveness toward her on the job had long ago begun to feel like shackles meant to hold her back from growing as an officer.

Until now…once again butterflies of excitement flew around inside her. She stared at the front door, waiting for her new partner to walk in.

She frowned as fellow officer Ryan Staub walked up and planted a hip on her desk. "So, the little lady is finally going to get to play at being a real cop," he said.

"First of all, I'm not a 'little lady' and second of all you're just jealous because I got the plum assignment of working with the new guy on the swamp murders."

His blue eyes darkened in hue. “I can’t believe Gravois is letting you work on that case. He must have lost his ever-loving mind.”

“He’s finally allowing me to work up to my potential,” she replied firmly. “Besides, you already worked the cases and nothing was solved. And get your butt off my desk.”

Ryan chuckled and stood. “Why don’t you go out with me for drinks on Friday night?”

She looked up at the tall, handsome blond man. “How many times do I have to tell you I’m not going out with you? I’ve told you before, I find you impossibly arrogant and you’re a womanizer and you just aren’t my type.”

He laughed again. “Oh, Sarah, I just love it when you sweet-talk me.” He leaned down so he was eye level with her. “Do you want to know what I think? I think you have a secret crush on me and you’re just playing hard to get.”

Sarah swallowed against a groan of irritation. “Don’t you have something better to do than bother me?”

He straightened up. “Yeah, I’ve got some things I need to get to.”

“Feel free to go get to them,” Sarah replied tersely. She released a sigh of relief as Ryan headed down the hallway toward the room where all the officers had their desks.

She and Ryan had known each other since they

were kids, but it was just in the last month or so that he'd decided she should be his next conquest. And he'd already had plenty of conquests with the women in town.

At thirty-three years old, she had no interest in finding a special man. She'd thought she'd found him once and that romance had gone so wrong. Still, if she was looking, Ryan would be the very last man on earth she would date.

At that moment the front door whooshed open and a tall, handsome hunk of a man walked in. She knew in an instant that it was *him*...the man Gravois had hired to come in and help investigate the four murders that had taken place.

She'd read his credentials and knew he had been a highly respected homicide detective with the New Orleans Police Department. His black hair was short and neat and his features were well-defined. A black shirt stretched across his broad shoulders and his black slacks hugged his long, lean legs. Definitely a hunk, and her new partner.

He approached her desk and offered a brief smile. Not only were his twilight-gray-colored eyes absolutely beautiful, but he also had thick, long dark lashes. "Hi, I'm Nick Cain, and I'm here to see Chief Gravois."

"Of course, I'll just go let him know you're here." She got up from the desk and headed down the hall to Chief Gravois's office.

It really made no difference to her that Nick Cain was a very handsome man. What she was most eager about was diving into the murder cases and perhaps learning something from the far more experienced detective turned private investigator.

She knocked on the chief's door and heard his reply. She opened the door and peeked inside. "He's here."

Gravois was a tall, fit man with salt-and-pepper hair and sharp blue eyes. "Get Shanks to sit on the desk and you bring him back here so I can talk to both of you at the same time."

Once again, an excited energy swirled around in the pit of her stomach. She opened the door behind which all the officers on duty sat. There were only three men in house at the moment, Ryan and Officers Colby Shanks and Ian Brubaker, who was the deputy police chief. "Colby, Gravois wants you on dispatch right now."

The young officer jumped out of his seat. He was a new hire and very eager to learn about everything. "Sure. Is the new guy here?" he asked as he followed just behind her.

"He is," she replied.

"Cool, I hope he's as good as he sounds."

"Let's hope so," she said.

They returned to the reception area where Nick Cain stood by the desk. "Sorry for the wait, if you'll just follow me, I'll take you to Chief Gravois."

"Thank you," he replied.

As she led him down the hall, she could feel an energy radiating from him. It was an attractive energy, one of confident male.

Suddenly Sarah wondered if her hair looked okay. Was the perfume she'd spritzed on that morning still holding up? She checked these thoughts, which had no place in her mind right now.

While she was working these cases with this man, she was a police officer, not a woman. Besides, one time around in the world of romance had been far more than enough for her.

She gave a quick knock on Gravois's door and then opened it. Nick followed her in and Gravois stood and offered his hand to him.

"Thomas Gravois," he said as they shook hands. "Please, both of you have a seat. It's good to have you here, Nick."

"Thank you, it's good to be here," Nick replied.

"Have you gotten all settled in at Irene's place yet?"

"I have," Nick replied.

"Okay then, first of all I want to introduce you to your new partner, Sarah Beauregard." Gravois pointed at her. "She will work side by side with you while you're here."

Nick nodded at her and Gravois continued. "Right now, you will be the only two working this investigation. If you need additional help then we can talk about that. I've set you two up in a small office that should have all you need. However, if there is something more that you want, please just let me know about it. In fact, I'll take you back there now and show you the setup."

The three of them stood and Gravois led the way down the hall to the office, which was really just an oversize storage area. A table had been set up in the center and a small filing cabinet hugged one of the corners. There was also a large whiteboard on one wall.

"I've put the murder books there in the center of the table, along with extra notepads for you to use. I'm sure you're eager to get started. I'm glad you're here, Nick. We need to get this guy off the streets as soon as possible."

"I hope I can help you with that," Nick replied.

"Later this afternoon I need to have a chat with you to finalize exactly how things are going to work," Gravois said. "I've also got some paperwork for you to sign."

"Whenever you're ready, sir," Nick replied.

"I'll just leave you to it and I'll check in with you later," Gravois said. He left the room and closed the door behind him.

Instantly the room felt too small. She could now smell the scent of Nick, a spicy intoxicating fragrance that she found very appealing. He gestured her toward a chair at the table and then he sat opposite her.

"Officer Beauregard," he began.

"Please make it Sarah," she said.

"Sarah, how long have you been with the police department?" he asked.

"I've been with the department for the past twelve years," she replied.

"Perhaps you have some insight into the murders?" He looked at her expectantly.

"Uh…to be honest, I haven't been involved in any of the investigations into the murders up to this point," she confessed.

He looked at her for a long moment and then released a heavy sigh. "So, what investigations have you been involved in during the last couple of years? I'm just trying to figure out here what I'm working with."

"You're working with a police officer whose sole desire and interest is to solve these four murders. I'm hardworking and tenacious and I'll have your back like a good partner should," she replied fervently.

His hard gaze on her continued. "I guess time will tell if you're really all that."

It was at that moment Sarah realized her new partner might just be a jerk.

Chapter Two

Nick walked back into Nene's house just before dinnertime. The house smelled of a delicious tomato-based sauce and freshly baked bread. He carried the four murder books up the stairs and placed them on the small table to look at later.

By the time he'd had a brief conversation with his partner, Gravois had called him back into his office for a lengthy discussion about how things would work with Nick hired on as a free agent within the department. There were several documents for him to sign as well.

Once their talk was finally over, Nick made the decision that he'd study the murder books tonight and then first thing in the morning he'd speak with Sarah about where to begin their investigation.

He went into the bathroom to wash up for dinner and as he did, thoughts of his new partner filled his head. She was no bigger than a minute. He would guess her at about five feet tall and no more than one hundred pounds soaking wet.

Her blond hair was short and curly and she could easily be dismissed as a piece of fluff, except for her bright blue eyes, which had shone with a hunger that he had immediately identified with.

He wasn't sure why she'd been partnered with him. The only reason he could think of was Gravois wanted two fresh sets of eyes on the case. And he didn't know why there weren't more officers assigned to the murder cases.

What irritated him as much as anything was the fact that he found his new partner extremely pretty, and the first time she'd smiled at him he'd felt a spark go off deep inside him, something he hadn't felt for a very long time and something he definitely intended to ignore.

He went back downstairs and into the kitchen. "Nick," Nene greeted him with a big smile. "I wasn't sure you'd make it for dinner tonight, but I'm so glad you did. Please, have a seat at the table."

He started to sit, but she quickly stopped him. "Oh, that's Ralph's seat. He's kind of a creature of habit and likes to sit in the same place every night."

"No problem, I'll just sit over here." Nick moved to the other place that was set for dinner. "Something smells really delicious."

"Swiss steak, I hope you like it. We didn't talk about your food likes and dislikes when we spoke earlier. Are there any allergies I need to worry about?"

She pulled a large pan from the oven and set it on the countertop where a hot pad awaited it.

"None, and the only thing I really don't eat is brussels sprouts."

"That makes two of us," she replied with a tittering giggle. "To me no matter how you dress them up, they still taste like dirt."

"I totally agree," he replied.

At that moment a tall, fit man entered the room. He had dark brown hair worn in a buzz cut and deep-set brown eyes. Nick rose from his chair and held out his hand. "You must be Ralph," he said. "I'm Nick."

Ralph's grip was firm. "Nice to meet you, Nick," he said as the handshake ended. The two men sat at the table. "I hear you're the man Gravois has brought in to solve these Honey Island Monster murders."

"That's the plan," Nick replied. "Do you have any theories about the murders?"

"Me? Nah, I didn't even know about them until just recently," Ralph replied.

How was that possible? How, in a town this size, did everyone not know about the murders? He could understand the first one not being talked about much, but when the second one had occurred, he would have thought everyone would be talking about them.

The dinner was delicious. The Swiss steak was nice and tender and there were also seasoned green beans, a gelatin salad and homemade rolls. Nene definitely knew how to cook.

Ralph did not attempt to engage Nick in any conversation while they ate; however, Nene filled what might have been awkward silences with chatter about the weather, the town and her plan to bake an apple coffee cake along with biscuits and gravy for breakfast the next morning.

"My biscuits and gravy are a favorite with Ralph, right?" she said as they were ending the meal.

"You know that's right," Ralph replied. "I could eat them every day for breakfast."

"Then I'm definitely eager to try them," Nick replied.

He was grateful that dinner went by quickly, as he was keen to get upstairs and dig into the murder books. When they were all finished eating, he picked up his plate to carry it to the sink.

"Stop right there," Nene said. "I take care of all the cleanup around here."

"And don't even try to argue with her," Ralph said. "She's a very stubborn woman."

"Ha, that I am. Now put that plate down and go on your merry way," Nene replied.

"Then I'll just say thank you and dinner was delicious," Nick replied.

"If you want a little nibble later, I always leave chips and crackers and other snacky stuff on the table overnight for you to help yourself," she said.

"Thanks, Nene, and, Ralph, it was good meeting you." With that said, Nick left the kitchen. He probably should have looked at the murder books with Sarah, but he'd wanted to study the material on his own first.

Once he reached his room, he beelined toward the table. He first grabbed one of the fresh notebooks that Gravois had provided for them. He opened the notebook and made sure he had a pen.

While he read the files, he intended to make his own notes on the cases. He picked up the first murder book, surprised by how thin it was. In fact, he'd been surprised by how thin they all were when he'd picked them up to carry home.

The first thing he saw inside the first book were the crime scene photos. The victim, Babette Pitre, had been found in the back alley behind the post office and town hall. In the photos it appeared her throat had been ripped out and her face held wounds that looked like a wild animal had tried to claw her features off.

The autopsy also indicated that she'd been stabbed three times in the abdomen and it was probably some sort of claw gardening tool that had ripped out her throat and marred her face.

There was also an injection site in her upper arm. The tox screen had come back showing a heavy dose of Xanax in her system. The same was true in all the other victims. It was obviously the way the killer had knocked out his victims.

According to the records the people who had

shown up at the crime scene were Gravois, Officers Ryan Staub and Ian Brubaker, the coroner, Douglas Cartwright, and his assistant, and somebody named Ed Martin.

Nick frowned as he set the photos aside and moved on to the actual investigation notes. There were only three interviews that had been conducted at the time, one with a Gator Broussard, another with Babette's mother and finally one with a man named Zeke Maloney. The interviews were short and contained nothing earth-shattering as far as information went.

He was shocked as he checked out the next three murder books and realized it appeared that very little had been done to actually investigate these killings. Why?

Was Gravois that incompetent? Lazy? What about the other officers in the department? Did they really believe enough had been done in an attempt to catch this killer? Nick couldn't believe how lacking the investigations had been.

He leaned back in his chair and stared out the window where darkness had fallen and the streetlights had come on. He hadn't expected this. He hadn't expected the investigations that were done already to be so shoddy…so lacking. He had expected much better police work than this. He released a deep sigh.

Instantly a picture of his new partner filled his head once again. She'd already told him she knew very little about the murders. He also hadn't missed the fact that she hadn't answered him when he'd asked what kind of investigations she'd worked on before.

So, basically, he had crap in the murder files and a partner who he suspected was green as grass. It was a perfect recipe for failure.

However, he now had a vision of the four victims also in his head and they deserved justice, so failure wasn't an option. The way those women had been killed indicated that there really was a monster somewhere in Black Bayou. The length of time between the killings had shortened, so another one could occur any day.

He finally left the table and got ready for bed. He wanted to be sharp and refreshed in the morning. He'd told Sarah to meet him at seven thirty and they definitely had their work cut out for them.

Nick arrived at the police department just after seven the next morning. He was fueled by a good breakfast of the best biscuits and gravy he'd ever tasted and several cups of Nene's strong coffee.

He went directly to the room that had been assigned to them. He set the murder books back on the center of the table and then moved to the whiteboard, where he wrote the names of the four victims at the top.

He was pleasantly surprised when Sarah walked in at seven fifteen. At least she was early rather than being late. “Good morning,” she said with a bright smile.

She was definitely very pretty, and once again an electric spark shot off deep inside him. Despite the fact that it was hot and humid outside, she brought in the very pleasant scent of spring flowers. It irritated him that he even noticed her scent.

“Back at you,” he said, apparently more gruffly than he intended as her smile instantly disappeared. “Feel free to start reading the murder books. I’ll be interested to get your thoughts.”

She sat at the table and picked up the first file. He watched her as she read it. To her credit, she flinched only a little bit as she saw the graphic photos of the victims. He also couldn’t help but notice that her eyelashes were thick and long. Damn, what in the hell was going on with him?

She flipped through the interviews and then looked up at him with a delicate frown. “Is there more to this?”

“Apparently not, and the other three are just as thin.” He joined her at the table.

“Surely there has to be more someplace,” she replied with a look of confusion.

“I asked Gravois when I arrived a few minutes ago if there was more information on the murders and he told me what we have is all there is.” He attempted to keep all the judgment from his tone, but some of it must have crept in.

Her cheeks turned a dusty pink. “Well, this is embarrassing.” She shoved the murder book aside. “This should be an embarrassment to the whole department.”

“I’m glad we agree about something. How do you feel about going into the swamp?”

“I don’t have a problem with it. I ran in the swamp when I was young. What about you?”

“The same. My mother worked as an attorney in New Orleans and many of the people she represented were from the swamp. It wasn’t uncommon for her to take me with her when she went to meet with some of her clients.” The back of his throat threatened to close up at the very thought of the swamp. He swallowed hard against his rise of anxiety as he thought about going into the dark bayou.

“So, is that where we begin things? In the swamp?” she asked.

He nodded. “I think we should start by speaking to Lisa Choate’s parents.” Lisa had been the last woman killed.

“I think that makes sense. That murder is still fairly fresh,” she replied.

“But before that, I’d like to take a look at the place where her body was found,” he added.

“That was behind the bank. So, are we ready to go?” She gazed at him with big blue eyes that simmered with anticipation.

“Ready,” he replied.

She stood. "I'll drive."

"Normally I drive," he said.

"It makes sense for me to since I'm sure I know my way around town better than you do." Her chin lifted as if ready to challenge him. It surprised him, the bit of sass she had in her.

"Okay, then you drive for today," he replied.

They left the room and headed toward the back door of the station, stopping only when another officer was coming their way.

He smiled at Nick. "Investigator Cain, I'm Officer Ryan Staub." He held out a hand and the two shook. "I just want to let you know that if you find Short-Stuff here to be lacking in any way, I'd be available to join your team and help you out."

"Jeez, Ryan, I definitely feel the bus wheels rolling over my back," Sarah replied drily.

"I'll keep that in mind, but I like my partner just fine," Nick said. "So far, I find her extremely intelligent and I know she's going to be a great asset to me going forward."

"Oh...okay," Ryan replied. "Well, let me know if you need more help."

"Will do," Nick replied, and then he and Sarah moved on down the hall and exited into the hot early-September morning.

"Thank you," Sarah said.

"Is he always such a jackass?" Nick asked.

She released a musical laugh that was quite pleasant on the ears. "Only on the days when he's not being a total jerk." She gestured toward a blue sedan parked in a space at the back of the building.

"Do your other officers often mention your…uh… small stature?" He'd been offended by Ryan on so many levels, especially as a fellow officer of hers calling her Short-Stuff.

"No, that's just Ryan," she replied. She unlocked her car doors with her key fob and he got into the passenger seat. The interior of the car smelled like her, that scent of fresh flowers he found so attractive.

What in the hell was wrong with him? It had been years since he'd noticed a woman's scent. Why now? And why his partner?

What he needed was to keep himself in check, solve these murders as quickly as possible and then get back to his life in New Orleans.

SARAH FELT UNACCOUNTABLY nervous as she took off from the parking lot and headed toward the bank. She'd initially written off her new partner as being a jerk, but then he had defended her to Ryan and now she wasn't so sure what to think about him.

He looked as hot today as he had the day before. Clad in black slacks and a short-sleeved gray shirt, and with his shoulder holster and gun in place, he exuded strong male energy.

Not that it mattered as long as they could work together well. More than anything else, Sarah wanted to prove herself to the rest of the department.

She wanted to show them all that she wasn't just a nothing who Gravois gave a job to because he felt sorry for her. She wanted to prove that she wasn't just good for answering the phone or giving out tickets. She was ready to earn her place as a valuable member of the team and this was finally her opportunity to do that. The last thing she wanted was to develop a crush on her partner and lose her focus.

It was a short drive to the bank, where she parked and they got out of the car. "Down this way," she said as she led him down the alley between the bank and Masy's dress shop. "She was found right around here." She pointed to the general area where the body had been discovered.

He stared at the ground and then gazed around the area. "No security cameras back here?"

"None, and there's also no lighting," she replied.

"So, the killer had to know this area well and was able to easily drop the body off and get out of the here fairly quickly without being seen."

"There aren't many people on the streets at two or three in the morning," she replied. "But the killer had to know that this was an ideal place to leave her because of the lack of surveillance and lights."

"You would think the bank would have security cameras all around it."

She smiled at him. "You're thinking like a man

from the city. Bank robberies just don't happen in Black Bayou."

He nodded. "Point taken."

He looked around the area for several more minutes and then gazed at her once again. "Let's head to the swamp and at least get a first round of interviews done by the end of the day."

Minutes later they were back in her car and headed to Vincent's, a grocery store located just before the swamp took over the land. One thing the murder book held were directions to Lisa's parents' shanty.

"How was it that you ran the swamp when you were younger?" he asked.

"The house that I grew up in backed up to the swamp," she explained. "My parents worked full time and I was left alone a lot. When I was about eight or nine, I met a few kids who lived in the swamp, so I would go in to visit with them. I found it to be a magical place, but by the time I was a teenager I gave up the swamp for other after-school activities."

"And you were never afraid in the swamp?" he asked curiously.

"Never. My friends taught me a lot about the dangers and I was probably too young and dumb to be afraid," she ended with a small laugh.

"So, what do you think? Is our killer from the swamp? Or is he somebody from town? Gravois seems to feel certain it's somebody from the swamp."

"I really don't have an opinion about it all right

now. I don't have enough information to make an educated call," she replied.

"And that's good police work," he replied. "It's important that we both keep open minds going into all this."

His words warmed her. She hoped he wouldn't realize just how inexperienced she was, that she wouldn't show him what a neophyte she really was in actually working to solve crimes.

"What made you quit the police department and go out on your own as a private investigator?" she asked. "And I'm sorry if I'm being too nosy."

"Not at all," he replied. "In a word, it was burnout. I was working twelve- to fifteen-hour days for years and finally I decided it was time for me to slow down a bit. I now pick and choose the cases I work on."

"Is there somebody waiting for you back home? A wife or a girlfriend?" Sarah instantly wanted to kick herself in the behind for asking the personal question. But she was definitely curious.

"Neither, I've pretty much always been married to the job. What about you? Do you have a significant other?"

"No, and I'm glad. I want to stay laser focused on these cases without any outside distractions."

"Then we're definitely on the same page," he replied.

She pulled into the parking lot of the small grocery store, where a trail leading into the vast swamp was nearby. A lot of the people who lived in the swamp parked their vehicles here, as the owner of Vincent's was very swamp friendly.

"This is it. According to the directions, Lisa Choate's parents live up this trail and to the right at the second fork," she said.

"Let's go and let's hope Abe and Emily Choate can give us some information about their daughter that will move the investigation along." He led the way as they entered the trail.

It had been years since Sarah had been in the swamp. As she followed behind Nick, she drew in the scents of mysterious flowers and fauna along with the underlying odor of decay. The heat that surrounded them seemed to magnify the scents.

Bugs buzzed around her head as little woodland creatures scurried away on either side of the trail. Spanish moss dripped down from the treetops in beautiful lacy patterns.

Despite the beauty, she was also well aware of the dangers of poisonous snakes and gator-infested pools of water and wild boar that roamed the area.

Thankfully, they encountered none of those things by the time they arrived at the Choates' shanty. Before they could cross the rickety bridge that led up to the front door, a man stepped outside the small, slightly listing home on stilts.

"Who are you?" he asked with obvious suspicion. "What do you want here?"

"Mr. Choate, I'm Sarah Beauregard with the Black Bayou Police Department and this is special agent Nick Cain. We'd like to come in and talk to you and your wife about Lisa."

The tall, shirtless man stood still for a long moment and Sarah wondered if he was willing to speak to them at all. He finally nodded his head. "Come in then."

Nick and Sarah crossed the bridge and Lisa's father ushered them into the small shanty. "They're here to talk about Lisa," he said to the woman who sat on the end of the sofa. She stood as a slash of deep grief filled her features.

"Please, have a seat," she said as she stepped aside and gestured to the sofa. She twisted her hands before her. "Can I get you something to drink?"

"No thanks," Nick said. "And we're so very sorry for your loss."

He and Sarah sat side by side on the sofa and Emily sat in a chair facing them while Lisa's father remained standing by the door as if ready to kick them out at any moment.

"She was such a good girl," Emily said as her dark eyes filled with tears. "Always happy, always smiling." She swiped at her eyes. "She didn't deserve what was done to her."

"None of the victims deserved it," Sarah replied

softly. "And we're going to work very hard to get justice for Lisa."

"Nobody else has been working too hard to catch this killer," Abe said in obvious disgust. "Four dead girls and still no answers."

"We're hoping to change that right now," Nick replied.

Nick took the lead in the questioning and Sarah made notes. For the next hour he asked questions about Lisa and her lifestyle. Her parents insisted that she wouldn't leave the swamp with just anyone, but somebody had led her out of the swamp and to her death.

It would help if they knew where the women had been killed. The place where their bodies were found had only been the dumping grounds. They had been killed elsewhere, but where?

Her parents didn't know of any town girls who had been friends with their daughter, but she did have a couple of close friends who lived nearby in the swamp. In fact, she had been coming home after having partied a bit with her friends when she had disappeared.

Sarah was impressed by her partner, who asked smart and pointed questions yet displayed a softness and compassion for the two grieving parents.

They finally got up to leave, but Abe stopped them at the door. "You better hope you find this killer afore I do," he said with dark narrowed eyes. "'Cause if I find him, I'll kill him and rip his throat out just like he done my baby girl."

"Understood," Nick replied.

They left the shanty but before heading away, they paused at the bottom of the bridge to talk about what they had just learned. "I didn't see any interviews of Lisa's friends in the file," Nick said.

"That's because there were none there," Sarah replied. Even as inexperienced as she was, she knew this was lousy police work. There should have been follow-up interviews with all of Lisa's friends.

She was completely embarrassed by the department. She was particularly embarrassed by the man who had given her a job so many years ago. She'd believed Gravois was better than this. She knew there were people in town who believed he was lazy.

Maybe he was or maybe as the chief of police in such a small town he really didn't know how to investigate serious criminal cases like these. Or had he not cared because the victims were from the swamp? All of these thoughts deeply troubled her.

"Shall we interview Hayley Duchamp while we're so close to where she lives?" she asked. Lisa's parents had given them directions to two of Lisa's closest friends' places.

"Sounds like a plan," he replied. "I'm honestly surprised the friends haven't been interviewed before now. They might have some information about Lisa that her parents didn't know." He started up the trail toward Hayley's family shanty.

There was a loud crack. A gunshot! Nick immediately took Sarah to the ground and covered her body with his. At the same time, she heard the path of the bullet as it whizzed through the leaves and slammed into the tree near where they'd been standing.

Chapter Three

Nick's heart pumped sheer adrenaline throughout his body as he quickly pulled his gun. He stared into the direction that the bullet had come from but he saw nobody. He'd already been on the very edge just being in the swamp and now this. What in the hell?

He looked down at Sarah, who was as still as a statue beneath him. "Are you okay?" he asked softly.

"I'm fine," she replied just as quietly, but he could feel the frantic beat of her heart against his and the tenseness of her entire body beneath him.

"Stay here and stay down," he said. He slowly rose up to a crouch and then raced forward, zigzagging among the trees and thicket toward the spot where he thought the shooter might be. He glanced over his shoulder and saw that Sarah had crouched up and had her gun out before her.

No other shots came and it was impossible to specifically locate exactly where the shooter might have been. Nick sensed the danger was over as nothing else happened, but he continued to crouch down as he made his way back to Sarah.

It was only when he reached her that they both finally stood. "What the hell was that all about?" he asked. "Is it possible the people who live around here don't like law enforcement?"

"I guess that's possible, or it's also possible somebody just warned us off our investigation," she replied.

"Did it work? Do you want to be reassigned?"

"Heck no," she replied, her eyes lit with blue fire. "This just makes me more determined than ever to go forward."

He gazed at her for a long moment, looking for any cracks in her composure. That bullet aimed at them would have shaken up the most seasoned professional, but she appeared to have taken it in stride. Either she had a good poker face or she was utterly fearless.

While he could appreciate the first quality, the latter could be deadly. A cop had to function with a healthy amount of fear to stay alive. His partner was still such an unknown commodity to him.

What he did know was beneath her blue uniform and despite her slender frame, she had some definite feminine curves. In the brief moments he'd been on top of her, his traitorous brain had registered that fact.

"Is this something we should call in?" he asked.

"Call in to who?" she asked, and then continued,

"It doesn't appear we need backup and we can't even be sure that bullet wasn't from somebody hunting in the area. Now that I really think about it, it's a bit too early for anyone to be that worried about what we're doing."

"The fact that there was only one shot and none following up makes me believe it was just some kind of a random thing. I say we go on to Hayley's place but we proceed with caution," he finally said.

Together they took off with their guns leading the way. They managed to interview not only Hayley, but also Lily Champueau, who was also a friend of Lisa's.

By that time, they decided to head back into the office and not only process what they'd learned that day, but also plan what they intended to do the next day.

Sarah now sat at the table while Nick wrote the names of Lisa's two friends on the whiteboard beneath Lisa's name. When he was finished, he joined her at the table.

"Both women agreed that Lisa had no boyfriends," he said.

"And that she would not just go off with a guy from town," Sarah added dispiritedly. "We didn't really learn anything new that helps us."

"No stone unturned," Nick replied. "Patience is the key here. This case isn't going to be solved overnight. I just really don't understand why more wasn't done on these cases at the time the murders occurred."

Sarah released a deep sigh. "It's probably because they were swamp women," she said. "I'll tell you a dirty little secret about this town. A lot of the people who live in town are very prejudiced against the people who live in the swamp. They believe the men there are all lazy and drunks, and the woman are all worthless sluts." Her cheeks dusted with color. "If it would have been four town women who had been murdered, I think the investigations would have been far more thorough."

"So, what's changed? Why was I brought in if they don't really care about solving these crimes?"

"Pressure from several influential businessmen who demanded answers about the murders and Gravois's fear of being recalled," she replied. "Things seem to be slowly changing with the newer generation. It's mostly the old guard who are still hanging on to the prejudices."

"Well, it's good if things are changing. If prejudice is what kept these murders from being solved that's a hate crime in and of itself." Nene had hinted at some of this when she'd first spoken to him, but she certainly hadn't laid it out in such stark terms. It ticked him off. All victims, no matter who they were or where they came from, deserved justice.

"I also think it's very possible that the officers involved in the case believe a swamp person is responsible and they've just been waiting for somebody to walk in and either confess to the murders or give up some information about the guilty person."

He frowned. "So instead of actively investigating, everybody has been just hanging around and waiting for the crimes to solve themselves."

"Nick, I swear I didn't know what had been done or not done as far as the investigations were concerned. I was kept away from all this. I'm seeing this all for the first time and it actually disgusts me." She looked so earnest as she held his gaze.

He released a deep sigh. "Okay, so we use what little information there is in the files and we forge ahead. I want to ask you about some of the people in the murder books."

"Okay, ask away," she replied. There was a small piece of green vegetation stuck in her golden strands of hair. He wasn't sure if he wanted to pick it out because it didn't belong there or if he just wanted to touch the hair that looked so silky and soft. Instead, he opened his notebook and tightly grabbed his pen.

"The first person is Ed Martin. According to the murder books, he was at each of the dumping grounds before the bodies were removed."

She frowned. "His father, Gustave, owns most of Main Street. Ed helps his father with his businesses and collects rent from all the store owners. He's married and he and his wife have one son who is around nineteen or twenty. But I can't imagine why he would be anywhere around the bodies or the crime scenes."

"And what about Gator Broussard? He was interviewed after the first murder, but the notes don't hold much of the conversation."

A small smile curved her lips, igniting that little flutter of something inside him. "Gator is about eighty years old and has lived in the swamp all his life. He is something of a character and he catches gators for a living."

"What would he know about the murders to warrant him being interviewed?" Nick asked.

"Gator knows most everyone who lives in the swamp and he usually has a handle on what's going on there," she replied.

"Definitely sounds like somebody we should reinterview," he said.

"I agree. If anybody knows anything at all about these murders it would be Gator."

"Then let's plan to talk to him in the morning. Finally, do you know Zeke Maloney? He was listed as a potential suspect because he was seen hanging out around Chastain's store the night Marchelle Savoie's body was found in the alley there."

Once again Sarah frowned. "Zeke is in his late thirties or early forties. He lives in one of the rooms at the motel and I think he's a heavy drug user."

"Do you know what kinds of drugs he's into?" he asked.

"No, I'm sorry but I don't," she replied. "But if I was to make a guess, I'd say either cocaine or meth."

Nick leaned back in his chair. "So, tomorrow we'll plan on interviewing those three men… Ed Martin, Gator Broussard and Zeke Maloney. At some point later I want to talk to Gravois about the fact that we were shot at. Whether it was a stray bullet from a hunter or something else, he should be made aware of that fact."

"I agree," she replied. "Do you want me to go with you when you speak to him?"

"I don't think that's necessary." He closed his notebook and looked at his watch. It was just a few minutes after five. "Why don't we go ahead and call it a day and we can pick up fresh in the morning. I'm sure we are going to have some late nights going forward."

They both got up from the table. "Then I'll see you in the morning," she said. Once she left the room, he sank back down at the table.

He hoped like hell that she hadn't noticed how absolutely terrified he'd been the minute he'd stepped foot in the swamp. The swamp had haunted his nightmares for years, so going into the dark, mysterious marsh today had been a real challenge. It had been a terrifying journey for him.

He hoped his partner had seen none of his internal battle between duty and fear. The last thing he would want was to appear weak in anyone's eyes, but especially to his new partner.

He still didn't know what kind of a partner Sarah was going to be, but already he found her damned distracting. Her beautiful smile felt like a gift each time she flashed it at him. Her eyes were the vivid color of sapphires and shone just as brilliantly.

She wore her uniform well. The light blue shirt emphasized the blue of her eyes and the navy slacks fit her like they'd been tailored to showcase her nice butt and slender legs. Her lips looked so soft and kissable.

Why didn't she have a boyfriend or a significant other? She was bright and pretty and he couldn't believe nobody in town would be interested in her.

And why in the hell was he sitting here speculating about her? He'd had many female partners through the years, but with none of them had he wanted to know anything about them outside of the job.

Something about Sarah was different and she had him more than a little bit out of his comfort zone. Starting tomorrow he had to get his head on straight where she was concerned.

SARAH JERKED AWAKE with her heart racing and adrenaline flooding through her veins. Frantically she looked around the room as she slowly came out of the nightmare that had awakened her in the first place.

She turned over and checked the time. Just a little past five. Instead of going back to sleep for another hour or so, she decided to go ahead and get up. She turned on the bedside lamp and got out of bed. She then went into the kitchen and fixed herself a cup of coffee.

As she sipped the hot brew, she thought about the nightmare that had jerked her awake. She'd been back in the swamp, tangled in the vines that held her captive while shadow people had been shooting at her. It was easy to figure out why she'd had the dream.

Being shot at the day before had scared the living hell out of her. She hoped her partner hadn't seen her abject fear and she'd played it off okay. The last thing she wanted to do was give him the impression she wasn't up to the job.

She stared out the nearby window where the morning sun was just beginning to peek over the horizon. She had bought this house four years ago after having lived in an apartment since her parents' deaths. It was a nice three-bedroom with a fenced-in yard.

She'd had such high hopes for a happy life at that time. She'd been engaged to Brent Williamson, a man she'd believed was her soulmate, and she was busy planning her wedding. That, along with all of her confidence as a woman, had been destroyed by a single image on his phone.

Instead of dwelling on thoughts of her past heartbreak, she finished her coffee and then headed for the shower. A half an hour later she was dressed, but it was still too early to go into the police station.

She made herself another cup of coffee and carried it into her living room and sank down on the sofa. While her bedroom was decorated in pink and white, this room was done in blacks and grays with bright yellow accents.

She also had a guest bedroom done in shades of blue and a room with a desk set aside as an office which she hoped to actually use now that she was officially investigating crimes.

As she sipped on her second cup, she couldn't help but think about Nick. She could usually figure out people fairly well, but she couldn't get a good read on him. She'd found him supportive yet standoffish. His gaze had alternated between a warm gray and a distant deep steel, all in the course of a single day.

He was a hot, handsome man who could become a total distraction if she allowed him to be. But she couldn't let that happen. All she wanted to do was prove herself to be a hardworking officer who could get the job done, somebody who had the respect of her coworkers.

And thinking about that, she realized it was time to go. Hopefully today they could find out something that would lead them closer to catching the killer.

The intense heat and humidity of the summer months had finally broken and today was supposed to be a more pleasant temperature in the low eighties.

Knowing they would be driving several places,

today she parked in front of the police station and entered through the front door.

"Good morning," she said to Ian Brubaker, who sat at the reception/dispatcher desk.

"Morning, Sarah," he replied. "Your partner is already here."

"Thanks, then I'll just head on back. Have a good day, Ian." Her stomach knotted up a bit with anxious energy as she walked down the hallway and anticipated seeing her partner again.

"Her partner," that's how she had to think about him in her mind. She didn't want to think about him being Nick, because Nick was a man she was very attracted to.

She hadn't really dated much in the last couple of years and it ticked her off a little that the first man she found appealing on all levels was strictly off-limits.

She opened the door to their little office and walked in. Nick was seated at the table. "I'm just going over the people I think we need to talk to today," he said as a greeting. He gestured her toward the chair opposite him.

Instantly she smelled the scent of him, a mixture of soap and shaving cream and the spicy cologne. This morning he wore a gray polo that perfectly matched the color of his eyes, and his usual black slacks.

However, his eyes appeared distant, bordering on cold as he read off the list of people for questioning and then looked at her. “Anyone you want to add for today?”

“No, your list sounds good to me,” she replied.

“Then let’s get moving,” he said, and stood.

She quickly got to her feet and followed him out of the office and down the hallway. “I’ll drive today,” he said once they were outside. “You can navigate from the passenger seat.”

She wasn’t about to argue with him, not in the mood he appeared to be in. He led her to a black sedan and after he unlocked the doors with his key fob, she slid into the passenger seat.

The interior smelled like him, a scent that instantly stirred her. She watched as he walked around the front of the car to get to the driver door.

Why couldn’t he have a paunchy stomach and sloped shoulders? Why couldn’t he smell like menthol rub and mothballs? That would have made it so much better, so much easier for her.

“I figured we’d start with Ed Martin this morning. I’m assuming he works out of an office?” He started his car.

“He does. His office is down a few blocks on Main Street,” she replied.

“Any self-respecting businessman should be in his office by this time of the morning, right?”

“You would think so.” She fastened her seat belt and they took off.

"Is there anything I should know about Mr. Martin before we go in to talk to him?"

"To be honest, I really don't know much about him other than what I already told you," she replied.

She couldn't help but notice that Nick's voice seemed brusquer today and she also couldn't help but wonder if she'd done something to somehow offend him. Or maybe he was just a moody person.

Just like she couldn't know whether the killer was from the swamp or from town because she didn't have enough information, the same was true about Nick. She just didn't have enough information about him to even hazard a guess as to what kind of a personality he might really have.

It took only minutes for them to pull up in front of Ed's office. The writing on the large window in the front announced the business to be Martin's Enterprises.

There was a small sign on the door that indicated the office was open. They got out of the car and Nick opened the door and ushered Sarah inside. A small bell tinkled overhead to announce their arrival.

There were several chairs in front of the window and Ed sat at a large desk. He rose as they walked in. He was a small man with jet-black hair. He had a neatly trimmed mustache and was dressed in a suit that was probably worth Sarah's salary for a month.

"Good morning," he said in greeting. He nodded at Sarah and then turned his attention to Nick. "Sir," he said as he held out his hand. "I don't believe we've met."

"Nick Cain," Nick replied, and the two men shook hands. "And I assume you know Officer Beauregard."

"Yes," Ed said with a nod to her. "Please, have a seat," Ed said, and gestured to the chairs right in front of his desk.

Sarah and Nick sat and Ed returned to his seat. "Now, what can I do for the two of you this morning?" Ed asked.

"We're in the process of investigating the murders of four women. In going over the files we noticed that you were present at each of the scenes where the bodies were found. Why were you there, Mr. Martin?" Nick asked bluntly.

Sarah would have sworn that Ed's face momentarily paled. He cleared his throat and leaned forward in his chair. "Mr. Cain, my father has invested heavily in the town of Black Bayou. He's now an elderly man who has health and mobility issues, and so I'm his ears and eyes out here on the streets. I told Chief Gravois that I wanted to be notified of anything that was happening in town."

"You realize your presence there was highly unusual," Nick replied. "You probably contaminated a crime scene just by being there."

"I stayed outside of the perimeter and was only there as an observer," Ed replied.

"It's still highly unusual and definitely not a good idea," Nick replied. "What's your son's name, Mr. Martin?" he asked.

Ed straightened in his chair. "Why? He has nothing to do with any of this. I know he has alibis for all the nights of all the murders."

"All I asked for was his name," Nick replied.

Even Sarah, as much as she was a beginner in all this, recognized that Ed's response had been strange and made her wonder about Ed's son.

"Gus...his name is Gus," Ed said reluctantly.

"Thank you," Nick replied. "We're just trying to keep our records clear. You'll be available should we need to speak with you again?"

"Of course," Ed said.

"We appreciate your time, Mr. Martin." Nick stood and Sarah did the same.

"I think he should be the first name on our suspect list," Sarah said the minute they got back in the car.

"He and his son," Nick replied as he started the engine.

"He definitely protested too much when you simply asked for his son's name. Is Daddy showing up at the scenes to make sure there is no evidence that might point to sonny boy's guilt?"

"Makes you wonder, right?" he replied. "Gus Martin is definitely somebody we need to speak to, and not with his father present. If he's over the age of eighteen then we can interview him without Daddy. Now, let's head on over to the motel and see what we can learn from Zeke Maloney. I know where the motel is. I passed it on the way into town."

"Okay, then navigation is officially off," she replied lightly.

They drove in silence for a couple of minutes. "Is there a big drug problem around here?" he asked, breaking the silence.

"Are there some people using here, yes. Is there a big drug problem here, definitely not," she replied.

"Have you ever wanted to try anything?" There was genuine curiosity in his question.

"Never." She hesitated a moment and then continued, "If I was ever going to use, it would have been in the weeks after my parents were killed. I was so grief-stricken in that time I could understand the need…the utter desire to numb the excruciating pain, but even then, I wanted nothing to do with drugs."

"How and when were your parents killed?"

"I had just turned twenty-one when they were killed in a head-on crash by a drunk driver," she replied. She was vaguely surprised that even after all this time, thoughts of her parents still brought up an edge of deep grief in her.

"I'm so sorry for your loss," he replied with a kindness in his tone that made her believe him.

"What about you? Have you ever used?"

"No, never had the desire to screw up my career, although there were several people on the force who I knew used."

It was as if the ice had been broken between them and any brusqueness that had been in his voice earlier was now gone.

"Were you close to your parents?" he asked.

"Very close. They were my best friends," she replied. "I still miss them very much." Sarah wanted to keep the conversation going, but at that time he pulled into the motel parking lot.

"Zeke lives in unit three," she told Nick.

The motel was a place of hopelessness and despair. The outside of the eight-unit structure was a dismal gray, made only worse by the intense weathering of heat and humidity.

There was a lot of history here. Years ago, in unit seven a young prostitute had been murdered in a crime that had shocked the town, especially when it was revealed that a highly respectable businessman had been responsible for the crime after an innocent man from the swamp had spent years in prison for the murder.

Beau Boudreau had returned to Black Bayou after his years in prison and had hooked up with his old girlfriend, Peyton LaCroix. Peyton was a criminal defense lawyer and together they had solved the crime and cleared Beau's name. Peyton was still working as a lawyer and Beau was making a name for himself in home construction and repair. They had rediscovered their love for each other and were now a happy couple.

Nick pulled up in front of unit three and parked. They got out of the car and Nick knocked on the door.

"Yo...yeah...coming," a voice yelled out. A moment after that the door flew open to reveal Zeke.

He looked at both of them, then frowned. "Oh... uh... I was expecting somebody else."

Zeke might have been a good-looking man at one time, but now his cheeks were hollow and his teeth were rotten and an air of unhealthiness clung to his slender frame.

"Hi, Zeke, my name is Nick Cain, and this is Officer Beauregard. We were wondering if we could come in and ask you a few questions."

"Questions about what?" Zeke reached up and worried a scab on the side of his face. He dropped his hand to his side and shot a glance over his shoulder.

"We have a few questions about the murders that have occurred. We aren't interested in anything more than that," Nick replied pointedly. Sarah knew he was assuring Zeke that they weren't interested in his drug use...at least not for today.

Zeke stared at Nick for a long moment and then released a deep sigh and opened his door fully. Nick stepped in and Sarah followed right behind him.

The room was steeped in squalor. The blankets

and sheets had been torn off the bed, displaying a dirty gray mattress. Used fast-food containers littered the floor and the top of the dresser. Flies sat on the old food wrappers, as if too full to fly.

"I'd invite you to sit, but there's really no place for you to do that," Zeke said. He bounced from one foot to the other. "I don't know what kinds of questions you want to ask because I don't know anything about the murders."

"What were you doing out on the streets on the night of June 23 around two in the morning?" Nick asked.

Zeke frowned and began to pick at his face once again. "I don't really remember that night in particular, but there are lots of nights when I just feel like getting out of this room. I like to wait to go at a time when there aren't any people around to look at me and judge me. So I often walk in the middle of the night, but I had nothing to do with those poor women."

"When you're out walking, do you ever see anyone else out and around?" Sarah asked. She did not intend to be a silent partner, and it was time she assert herself just a little bit.

Once again Zeke frowned. "I've seen Ed Martin a couple of times and Officer Ryan Staub and Chief Gravois out and about once or twice. I've also met up with Dwayne Carter a few times. He's a friend and we just hang out together."

"Is there a reason you hang out with your friend

that late at night?" Nick asked. Sarah knew the reason. Dwayne Carter was the local drug dealer.

"Uh…we're just both night owls, I guess."

"Did you see or hear anything that particular night that might have looked or sounded suspicious?" Sarah asked.

"No, not that I remember."

"Then you had no idea that Marchelle Savoie was dead in the alley next to where you and your friend were hanging out," Nick said.

"God no," Zeke replied. "I didn't find out about her murder until the next day. Look, I'll admit I'm a dope addict. I shoot and snort a lot of stuff, but I'm not a killer." He shook his head. "No way, nohow could I ever kill anyone."

"I think he's a dead end," Nick said minutes later when they were in his car and headed toward the swamp.

"I agree." She cast him a quick glance. "I hope I didn't irritate you by jumping in with some questions."

"Not at all. I want you to feel free to do that with anyone we interview. We're partners, right?" He cast her what appeared to be a genuine, warm smile.

"We are," she agreed. As he focused back on the road, she stared out her side window and again fought the wonderful warmth his smile had evoked inside her.

Nick seemed to have a split personality where she

was concerned. One minute he was cool and distant and the next warm and engaged.

When he was warm and engaged, she found herself wanting to be his partner…his best friend and lover. She sat up straighter in her seat as the word…the very thought of *lover* whispered through her head. She hadn't been with anyone since Brent, hadn't even thought about a lover until now.

Nick had been nothing if not professional with her and she had absolutely no reason to believe he was into her in any kind of a sexual way. Still, she swore there was something between them, some snap in the air…a momentary absence of breath and a palpable energy she found very hard to ignore as it enticed and excited her.

She'd be a fool to allow these thoughts any more oxygen in her brain. Nick was here to do a job and not to play cozy with his partner, and it was in Sarah's best interest to remember that.

Chapter Four

Nick tried to keep his attention off Sarah as they drove to Vincent's, where he parked the car. "Do you know where this Gator lives?" he asked once they were out of the car.

"Not specifically, but from what I've been told he's most always around and all we really have to do is go in a little ways and holler for him," she replied.

He looked at her in open amusement. "If we go in there and yell Gator, I hope that isn't a wake-up call to all the alligators in the area."

She laughed, those same musical tones that he found so attractive. He'd tried to keep cool and aloof from her. He was sorry to learn about the tragedy of her parents' deaths. He hadn't wanted to know anything about her personal life. But now he did and despite any notion to the contrary, he found himself wanting to know more about her.

Surely it wouldn't hurt if they became friends as they worked together, he told himself. It was the thought of friends with benefits he didn't want… couldn't entertain.

They walked into the mouth of the marsh with their guns drawn as a precaution. As it had yesterday, his heart beat faster than normal as a wealth of anxiety knotted in his stomach and tightened his chest.

You'll be fine, he told himself. *You're an adult and you have a gun. The swamp can't hurt you.* He said the words over and over again like a mantra. It was his effort to still the irrational fear that pressed so tight against his chest.

They hadn't gone far when they came upon a large dead fallen tree trunk. They stopped there. "Gator Broussard," Sarah yelled in a surprisingly strong voice that sent birds flying from the tops of several nearby trees. They stood still and waited. After several moments had passed, she yelled for him again.

"I'm here, what's the damn fuss all about?" The old man seemed to magically appear from the thicket to their left.

Gator was clad in a pair of jeans held up at his slender waist by a piece of rope. A gray T-shirt stretched across his narrow shoulders. His hair was nearly white and his tanned face was weathered with wrinkles. He also leaned on a cane. But his eyes shone with not only a deep intelligence, but also a sparkling humor.

"Mr. Broussard, I'm Nick Cain." He held out his hand to the old man.

Gator gave it a firm shake. "Well, ain't you the fancy one shaking my hand and all." Gator looked at Sarah. "And look who it is…little Sarah Beauregard all grown up."

"Hi, Gator," Sarah said with a smile.

"Mr. Broussard, we'd like to ask you some questions," Nick said.

"Gator, son. Make it Gator, and what do you want to talk to me about?"

"Is it possible we could go to your house so we can discuss some things with you in private?" Nick asked.

He wanted to go to Gator's place because they were still hunting for the killing grounds. While there was no way he believed a man as old and as thin as Gator had killed those women and transported them into town, they would at least be able to positively exclude his place.

"I suppose I could take you home with me, but I gotta warn you, it ain't company-ready," Gator replied. Without saying another word, he turned and headed up the narrow trail.

Nick gestured for Sarah to go before him, and so she fell in just behind the old man and Nick brought up the rear. Despite the use of the cane, Gator scampered fairly nimbly through the thicket.

As they went deeper in, pools of dark water lined their way and the trail narrowed. Bugs buzzed around Nick's head and a slight edge of claustrophobia and apprehension tightened all the muscles in his entire body. The tree limbs pressed so tight into the trail and the thick underbrush seemed to be reaching out for him.

Suddenly he was five years old again and he was hopelessly lost in the dark and scary swamp. The waters were filled with huge gators that gnashed their jaws in the anticipation of eating him. The Spanish moss clung to his head and tried to blind and suffocate him. He wanted out. God, he needed to get out.

Thank God at that moment a small shanty appeared and snapped him out of his dark memories. He wasn't a little kid anymore and he had important work to do.

A rickety narrow bridge led up to the front door. Gator raced across it and threw open the door and the two officers followed him inside.

It was a small structure with another single door that Nick assumed was his bathroom. A single cot obviously served as his bed and sofa and a potbellied stove looked dirty with use. There was only one other chair in the room, an old, broken recliner.

"I warned you it wasn't company-ready," Gator said. "Go ahead and have a seat." He gestured them toward the cot and then he sat in the recliner. "I suppose you're here about the murders."

"We are," Nick replied.

"What makes you think I know anything about them?"

"Gator, you know most all of the people who live here in the swamp. You know where they go and what they do. You would know if any of the men here are capable of committing such horrid crimes," Sarah said.

"I told Gravois when he first came around asking questions after the first murder that I didn't think a man from the swamp was the killer and nothing since then has changed my mind. My gut instinct tells me this is the work of somebody from town and my gut instinct rarely steers me wrong." His eyes darkened.

"What?" Nick asked. There seemed to be more that Gator wanted to say. "Gator, is there something else on your mind? Something you want to say?"

Gator frowned. "There is one man here in the swamp...name is James Noman. He lives in a shanty deep in and nobody knows much about him. Word is he's a bit touched in the head and folks steer clear of him."

"Sounds like somebody we should talk to," Nick replied. "Can you tell us how to find his shanty?"

"I don't think I can tell you, but I suppose I could show you," Gator said with a bit of reluctance in his tone.

"Can you show us now?" Sarah asked.

"We would really appreciate it if you could," Nick added.

Gator rose to his feet and she and Nick did the same. Could it be this easy? Was it possible this James Noman was the person they sought?

They left Gator's place and headed down a trail. Once again Gator moved quickly as they navigated over tubers and under branches. More water appeared on either side of them as the trail narrowed.

Nick lost track of time as he focused solely on staying on the trail, which had now nearly disappeared, and the direction that they were going in. The sunlight that had shone through the branches overhead earlier had faded. It was no longer feasible to see through the heavy canopy of leaves.

The air grew much cooler and a cacophony of sound filled his head. Fish jumped and slapped in the waters and strange birdcalls came from the trees.

He had never been this far into the swamp before and there was an air of deep mystery here that had him on edge. This was sheer torture for him. He had to keep reminding himself that he wasn't that lost little kid anymore. He was now an adult…with a gun and a desperate need to solve these murders.

Finally, Gator came to an abrupt stop. He pointed straight ahead where a shanty was almost hidden by the tupelo and cypress trees that surrounded it.

"That's Noman's place." Gator turned to look at them. "And this is as far as I go." Nick could have sworn there was a touch of fear in the old man's eyes.

"Thanks, Gator. We'll take it from here," Nick said with forced confidence.

Gator stepped aside so she and Nick could go ahead of him. "If you get lost on the way out, just holler for me." He quickly turned and headed back the way they had come. Nick took the lead, with his gun held tight in his hand as they slowly approached the small shanty.

From the outside, the place appeared completely abandoned. There was nothing on the porch and one of the side windows was broken out. The bridge that led to the place was narrow and missing several of its old boards.

"Mr. Noman," Nick yelled when they reached the foot of the bridge. They waited and listened for a response. After several seconds had ticked by, Nick hollered again, but there was still no answer.

"He must not be home," Sarah said. Nick thought he heard a touch of trepidation in her voice. He felt more than a little uneasy as well.

They had no idea what they were getting into here. Gator had mentioned that Noman was touched in the head. What exactly did that mean? Dealing with somebody who had mental issues was always concerning and sometimes dangerous.

"Maybe we should go up and knock on his door," Nick said. And maybe they could get a peek in his windows and see what might be inside.

"Okay," Sarah replied.

He tucked his gun back into his holster to navigate the narrow, hazardous bridge. Once he was on the other side, he pulled his gun once again and watched as Sarah slowly came across.

Once she was by his side, he turned and knocked on the door. "Hello?" he called out. "Is anybody here? Mr. Noman? Are you there?"

There was a thick scent of decay around the small structure that instantly raised the hackles on the back of Nick's neck. It wasn't the smell of vegetation decay, but rather it was the odor of animal or human rot.

"Do you smell that?" Sarah asked softly.

"I do," Nick replied.

He walked up to the door and knocked. All of his muscles tensed. He had no idea what to expect, but the smell alone raised all his red flags.

As a homicide detective, he'd smelled this offensive odor far too many times in the past. So, what was going on around here? What was Noman doing in this isolated shanty?

He knocked once again on the door and still there was no response. "He's either not here or he's not answering." More than anything he wanted to just open up the door, but there were rules about things like that and working with a cop as his partner, he had to abide by the rules. Besides, if this was their killer, he didn't want to do anything that would mess up a prosecution.

Thankfully, at the moment his abject fear of the

swamp was usurped by the desire to get some answers.

"So, what do we do now?" Sarah asked.

"I want to get a peek in the windows," Nick replied. He walked around on the narrow porch and reached the broken window. One glance inside showed him nobody was in the place.

There was a cot half-covered in a raggedy, torn quilt and a potbellied stove. Nick stared in shock at the walls, which were covered in bones. Large bones and smaller ones, Nick was unable to identify what kind of bones they were. Were any of them human?

His gaze caught and held on one corner of the room. Blood. Old blood and fresh blood, it spattered the walls and pooled on the floor.

Was this the killing place they'd been looking for?

SARAH AUDIBLY GASPED as she saw the bones and the blood inside the shanty. Without thinking, she tightly grabbed hold of Nick's forearm. "Is…is it possible this is the place where the women were all killed?"

"Anything is possible at this point," he replied. "I'd like to get inside and get a closer look at those bones and the blood."

She withdrew her hand from his arm, deep inside registering the warmth of his skin and the play of taut muscle beneath. "What now?" she asked.

"We head back and see if we can get a search warrant for this place." Frustration was rife in his tone. She had a feeling if she wasn't with him, he would have gone on inside. But that would screw up the prosecution who would want a clean, by-the-book investigation.

They each crossed back over the bridge. "Do you know how to go back or do we need to yell for Gator?" she asked. She certainly had no idea how to get them out of here. She'd been too focused on not falling off the narrow trail and into the gator-infested waters.

"I can get us back," Nick replied. "I paid special attention as to where we were going so I could get us back without Gator's help."

"Thank God," Sarah replied.

There was a sudden loud rustle coming out of the brush next to them. Sarah caught the flash of a slender, bare-chested man darting down the trail in front of them.

"James Noman," she yelled, and took off after him. He jumped over a pool of water and plunged into the thicket on the other side. She hesitated only a moment before leaping over the water, grateful to land on soggy marsh. "James, stop. We just want to talk to you."

She desperately wanted to catch him for questioning. She also desperately wanted to prove herself to Nick. Tree limbs tore at her as she ran by them as fast as she could to keep up with him. She was vaguely aware of Nick following close behind her.

Her heart pounded and her breaths came in deep gasps as she struggled to keep up with the man she knew was James Noman. He zigged and zagged through the brush and Sarah remained on is heels.

"James, please," she gasped out. "We just want to talk to you."

Like a gazelle, he leaped over another large pool of water.

This time she didn't hesitate and jumped after him. She didn't make it to the other side and instead plunged into the shoulder-deep water. She instantly tossed her gun to the trail and then gasped and flailed, momentarily shocked by the unexpected plunge.

Her heart exploded in fear as she thought of all the alligators that might be close to her. She tried to calm herself and then struggled to get out.

It wasn't until Nick offered her a helping hand that she was finally able to get her footing again and get out of the water.

By that time Noman had disappeared. "Damn," she exploded in sheer frustration. She wasn't mad only that they'd lost their suspect, but also by the fact that she now stood before Nick like a drowned rat. So much for impressing him with her prowess.

"We'll try to get him tomorrow," he said. "Let's get you back to the car. I have a towel in my trunk."

"Thanks," she replied, grateful that he took the lead so she could do her walk of utter shame behind him.

She shivered several times from being soaked in swamp water. Damn, why hadn't she judged the jump better? She felt like a total fool in front of the man she had most wanted to impress.

It seemed to take forever for them to finally get back to Nick's car in Vincent's parking lot. He opened his trunk and inside was not only a towel but there were also bottles of water, a box of energy bars and a kit for collecting evidence.

"You look like you're prepared for everything," she said.

"I'd like to tell you I was a Boy Scout in my youth, but the truth is I just like to try to make sure I have what I need to survive should I get stranded somewhere." He handed her the towel.

"Thanks." She ran the fluffy towel over her body, trying to get as dry as possible, and then placed the towel on the passenger seat and got into the car.

He closed the trunk and slid behind the steering wheel. "If you give me directions to your place, I'll take you there so you can change clothes."

"I appreciate it, and I'm really sorry, Nick." She felt so miserable about this. She should have judged the jump before leaping. Now they were having to take time out of their busy day for her stupid mistake.

"Don't beat yourself up about it," he replied. "I appreciate the effort you gave it."

"I'm just glad a gator didn't get me."

"Trust me, I wouldn't have let that happen. I've

never lost a partner yet and I don't intend to start with you." He shot her a surprisingly warm smile. "So you're stuck with me."

"I'm surprised you want to be stuck with me," she replied. She released a deep and miserable sigh. "In case you haven't noticed yet, I'm totally inexperienced when it comes to investigations like this. I've been stuck on desk duty and handing out speeding tickets for the last twelve years of my career."

"To be honest, I kind of guessed as much," he said.

"I'll understand if you prefer to ask for another partner. Ryan has certainly indicated he'd like to work with you and Ryan is far more experienced than I am." She half held her breath for his reply.

"Nah, I'm good with you. On a positive note, I think you have really good instincts and besides, this way I can teach you how to conduct a murder investigation the proper way."

She released a dry laugh. "Then that will make me the only person in the department who can investigate properly. Turn left at the next street," she instructed him.

"Got it," he replied.

"All I can smell right now is nasty swamp." She plucked at her wet shirt. "At least I managed to keep my gun out of the water, but I hope your car doesn't smell bad once I get out of it."

He laughed. "That's the last thing I'm worried about."

A shiver raced up her spine. This time it wasn't from her damp clothes but rather because of the deep, delicious sound of his laughter.

"Make a right here," she said. For the second time, she felt like the ice had truly been broken between them. If all it took for him to share a laugh with her was for her to jump in the swamp, then she'd do it every day.

"My house is the fourth one on the left," she said.

He pulled up in her driveway. "Nice place," he observed.

She looked at the house that sported gray paint and black trim. The lawn was neatly trimmed and two wicker chairs sat on her front porch with bright red cushions. "Thanks. Are you waiting for me? My car is at the station."

"Sure, I'll wait," he agreed.

She turned in her seat to look at him. "Please, Nick, come on inside. I don't want you having to sit out here in the car when my sofa is pretty comfortable." She opened the car door, relieved when he opened his as well.

Together they approached the front door. She unlocked it and then gestured him inside. Nick was the first man to be in her house since her breakup with her fiancé. But he wasn't here for a visit, she reminded herself. He was here because of her own stupidity. God, she felt so dumb.

"Please, make yourself at home and I'll be out as

quick as I can," she said, and then headed for her bedroom. Once there she stripped off her wet clothes and started the shower.

Within minutes she stood beneath the warm spray and washed all the swamp off her, chasing the nasty smell away with her fresh-scented soap.

She was still confused about her feelings toward Nick. The more they spent time together, the stronger her physical attraction to him grew. Even when he'd grabbed her hand to pull her out of the water, an electric current of pleasure had raced through her at his touch.

Still, it was thoughts of Nick waiting for her that made her not dawdle. She got out of the shower, dressed in a clean uniform and then took a couple of minutes to blow-dry her hair. She spritzed on her favorite perfume and then left her bathroom.

When she returned to the living room Nick stood in front of her wall of photographs. There were pictures of her with her parents and her with Gravois. She also had photos of herself with two of her girlfriends, girlfriends she'd neglected for the past couple of weeks.

He turned when she came in the room and offered her a smile. "I'm assuming these are your parents," he said, and pointed to a picture that had been taken when she was twelve years old.

"You'd be assuming correctly," she replied. She stepped up next to him. "Are your parents still alive?"

"They are," he replied. "When I'm back home my mother insists I have dinner with them at least once a week."

"That's nice. And what about siblings? Do you have any?"

"I have a sister who is two years older than me and a brother who is two years younger," he replied.

"And are you all close?"

"We are," he replied. "What about you? Any siblings?"

"No, I've got no family." A hunger filled her, the hunger that had been with her for a long time. It was the desire to have somebody in her life in a family kind of way. But at this point in her life, she wasn't really looking for anybody.

She'd thought she had found that with Brent, but that had ended up being nothing but a heartache and now she was reluctant to ever try romance again.

"There are days I'd gladly share my brother with you," Nick said with a touch of humor in his tone. "He teases me unmercifully and is a real pain."

She laughed. "I'd like to see that. Shall we go?"

"Yeah, I just realized it's almost six, which means I'm too late for dinner at Nene's place. I was wondering if you'd like to go to the café for a quick dinner. We can talk about things while we eat."

"Yeah, okay," she replied. She hadn't realized how late it had become and she was definitely surprised by his offer. It was nothing more than a business dinner, she told herself as she followed him back out to the car.

So why did she wish that it was something different? Why did she wish it was a real date?

Chapter Five

Once again Nick found himself fighting off a simmering desire for his partner. It had begun again the moment he had pulled her out of the water. Her wet uniform had clung to her body and shown off all her curves.

It wasn't just that. It had also been how quickly she'd responded to seeing the man on the trail and her bravery in taking the leap that had landed her in the water.

It had also broken his heart more than a little bit for her when he'd heard the haunting loneliness in her voice when she'd spoken of having no family at all. At that moment all he'd wanted to do was draw her into his arms and hold her tight.

Now in the small confines of his car, it was her scent that drove him half-dizzy with the desire to pull her close to him and taste the sweetness of her lips.

Jeez, what in the hell was wrong with him? He hadn't felt drawn to a woman in the last three years.

Why now and for God's sake why her? Somehow, he was definitely going to have to try to keep himself in check.

"Have you eaten at the café before?" she asked.

"No, not yet. Is the food good there?"

"I think it's excellent," she replied. "How is Nene's food?"

"Very good. She'd an amazing cook. Do you cook or do you eat out a lot?" he asked.

"I rarely eat out. I like to cook, although there are nights when I'm too tired and I just throw something in the microwave. What about you?"

"Other than eating with my family one night a week, I cook for myself. My mom made sure all of us kids knew how to cook when we were teenagers."

"Smart woman," she replied.

"She told us it was a life skill that we all needed to know to survive on our own."

By that time, he had pulled into the parking space behind the café. He cut the engine and then the two of them got out of the car.

"Nice evening," he observed as they walked around to the front door of the place. The temperature was pleasant and the skies were clear with the sun slowly drifting down in the sky.

"It's beautiful out," she agreed.

He opened the front door and ushered her in before him. Once inside he looked around with interest. It was the usual setup for a café with booths along the two outer walls and a row of tables down the middle.

The walls were painted yellow, but two of them held what appeared to be really nice hand-painted murals. One was of Main Street and the other was of cypress trees dripping with Spanish moss.

The scents inside were positively wonderful. They were of simmering meats and savory sauces. There was also a sweetness in the air that made him think the desserts here might be terrific.

He was vaguely surprised by how many people were dining on a Thursday night, definitely a testament to how good the food must be. He spied an empty booth near the back and guided her there.

"Is this okay with you?" he asked.

"It's fine with me," she replied, and slid into the seat. He slid in across from her and picked up one of the menus that were propped up between the tall salt and pepper shakers.

It didn't take long for a waitress wearing the name tag of Heidi to come to wait on them. "Can I start you two off with something to drink?" she asked.

"I'll take a sweet tea," Sarah said.

"Make that two," he added.

"Are we ready to order some food? Or do we need more time?" Heidi asked.

"I'm ready to order. I'll have the bacon burger with fries," Sarah said as she placed the menu back in place.

"And I'll have the shrimp platter," he said.

"Okay, let me get those orders into the kitchen and I'll be back with your drinks."

As she moved away from their booth, he put his menu back in place and then leaned back in the seat. "Let's talk about today," he said. He needed this to be a business dinner, otherwise it would feel too much like a date and the last thing he wanted to do was to date his partner.

"Where do you want to start?" Sarah leaned forward, her beautiful blue eyes filled with that hunger to learn, a look he found incredibly sexy.

"Let's start with Zeke. Even though it's obvious the man has a bad drug issue, that's one reason why I'm reluctant to pull him off the suspect list," he said.

"Who knows what kind of drug-induced delusions he might suffer and what might he do when in those delusions?"

"Exactly," he replied. He liked that she always seemed to know what was in his mind. "In my gut do I believe he's our guy? No, but I think we need to keep him on our suspect list until we interview him another time."

"I totally agree," she replied.

The conversation paused for a moment as Heidi delivered both their drinks and their food. His shrimp platter included both scampi style and fried shrimp. It also had slaw and garlic bread and it all looked and smelled delicious.

"Now let's talk about the elephant in the room," he continued.

"When you drop me off back at the office, I'll type up the paper requesting the search warrant for Noman's place. Hopefully we'll have it by sometime tomorrow afternoon."

"Good. I can't wait to get in there and check out both the bones and the blood. Have there been any missing women reported in the past?" he asked. If any of those bones belonged to women, then those women had to have come from somewhere.

"Not that I've heard about." She took a big bite of her burger. He appreciated the fact that she could eat while they talked about blood and bones. That was another mark of a good cop.

She chewed and then swallowed. "However, that doesn't mean girls haven't disappeared from the swamp and it just hasn't been reported."

He frowned. "I guess I don't have to ask why it wouldn't be reported."

"I'm sure the people from the swamp have lost all belief in the police department," she replied. "They have to recognize that little to nothing was done to investigate the murders of those young women."

For the next two hours they ate and talked about not only these particular crimes, but also some of the cases he had worked on in the past as a homicide detective.

She was an apt listener, stopping him only to

ask questions. It was a new experience for him to talk with somebody who was actually interested in what he was saying. Amy had never wanted to hear about his work.

"I'll share with you one more story and then I'll shut up," he said as he realized he'd monopolized much of the conversation.

"Please, keep sharing," she replied. "I'm enjoying this and I'm learning so much."

"Let's order some dessert and coffee," he replied. Once he got Heidi's attention, he ordered a piece of caramel apple pie and Sarah got a piece of chocolate cream pie. They both got coffee and then he continued with the last story he intended to share with her.

"When I was a rookie cop, I got involved in a foot chase. We were after a guy who had committed the armed robbery of a convenience store. He'd already tossed his gun away so I knew he was unarmed. I really wanted to be the one to catch him, to prove myself worthy to the rest of the more seasoned officers that were with me."

"I know that feeling well," she replied with a rueful smile. God, she had a beautiful smile.

He took a drink of his coffee and then continued. "Anyway, I was running as fast as I could and he eventually darted into a clothing shop that had an open-air doorway. At least I thought it was completely open-air until I ran face-first into a pane of glass."

"Oh no," she gasped, her eyes wide.

He laughed. "Oh yes. I not only shattered the glass but I also broke my nose and my pride."

She laughed, that beautiful sound that reached in and somehow touched his soul. "I'm so sorry, I don't mean to laugh."

He grinned at her. "It's perfectly okay to laugh."

To his surprise she reached across the table and touched the back of his hand, shooting a rivulet of warmth through him. "Thank you so much for sharing that with me."

She pulled her hand back from his and picked up her fork and he immediately missed the warmth of her touch. As they ate their desserts, they talked about their plans for the next day.

"First thing in the morning we'll go back to the swamp and try to make contact with Noman again," he said.

"And after that?" she asked.

"I'd like to talk to Zeke once again and ask him about alibis for the nights of the murders. I'd like to see if we can either exclude him for sure from the suspect pool or keep him on."

"And maybe we need to catch up with Ed Martin's son and see if he has any alibis for the murders," she added.

"Absolutely," he agreed. "I find Ed Martin's reason for being at the crime scenes very sketchy. If he wants to stay up on what's happening in town, a simple phone call to or from Gravois would have sufficed. He didn't need to be at the scenes."

"I completely agree."

By that time, they had finished their desserts and coffee. "I guess we should get out of here," he said with a bit of reluctance. He'd enjoyed the food, but what he'd really enjoyed was the conversation and just looking at her across the table.

He motioned to Heidi for their bill. Sarah insisted she pay her own way and although he would have been perfectly fine to pay for them both, they wound up splitting the tab.

Night had completely fallen and the moon was nearly full in the sky. Now that they were out of the restaurant, he could smell the sweet flowering scent of her again. It tightened the muscles in his stomach, pulling forth a desire he desperately fought against.

She smiled up at him. "I hate to say this, but talking about murder sure gave me a big appetite."

He laughed. "That just means you're a good cop."

Her smile faltered as she held his gaze intently. "I'm not a good cop yet, but I'm definitely determined to become one."

They got into his car and he headed toward the police station where hers was parked. "I'm going to sleep good tonight," she said. "My tummy is so full, it's the end of the day and I'll definitely sleep well."

"That makes two of us," he agreed.

"My car is in the back parking lot," she said as he approached the station.

He pulled around back and her car was one of three in the dark lot. "I'm just going to head inside and get that paperwork done for our search warrant," she said as she unbuckled her seat belt.

"Do you need any help with that?" he asked.

"No, I think I've got it." She got out of the car and he did as well.

"I'll walk you to the door," he said, unsure what motivated him to do so.

"Okay," she agreed. "So, what time do we start in the morning?"

"Why don't we keep it at seven thirty," he said.

They reached the back door and she turned to face him. The moonlight caressed her pretty features. As she smiled up at him all he could think about was kissing her. Her lush lips seemed to call to his and he leaned forward.

It was only when he saw her eyes widen slightly that he snapped back in place, horrified by what he had been about to do. "Good night, partner. I'll see you in the morning." He turned quickly on his heels and walked back to his car.

SARAH WENT THROUGH the back door, her heart beating wildly in her chest. Had he been about to kiss her? She could swear she saw a flicker of desire in his eyes as he'd leaned toward her.

In that brief moment in time, she'd so wanted him to kiss her. She'd wanted to feel his lips against her own. She'd wanted him to pull her against his body and hold her tightly against him.

She headed to their workroom where her computer sat at the desk waiting for her. She had decided that morning to start bringing her computer with her each day, anticipating the time when something like a search warrant would come up. She'd also been keeping notes on it about the investigation.

She logged into her official account and searched to find the appropriate form. Once she found it, she began the process of filling it out.

Thankfully, about a year ago the department had paid to get things streamlined and online for the officers. Normally a search warrant would not be considered by a judge if it was without a senior officer on the application. However, she added Nick's name to the request and hoped Judge Harry Epstein would grant it.

She emailed the form to the judge and then closed down her computer and packed it up to carry home. Hopefully, they would hear something back on the warrant by tomorrow afternoon.

Minutes later as she walked back to her car, she thought about the evening that had just passed. There had been moments when it hadn't felt like a business dinner at all, but rather like a date.

She had loved hearing about his past cases and it

had been especially kind of him to share the story of him running into the door and breaking his nose. She knew he'd told it to her in an effort to make her feel better about landing in the swamp waters.

She definitely was developing a mad crush on her partner and she couldn't stop thinking about that single breathless moment when she'd believed he was going to kiss her.

Did he feel it, too? That snap of electricity? That surge of warmth in the room whenever they were together? Had the desire she thought she'd seen in his eyes tonight just been a trick of the moonlight or had it been real? Only time would tell.

She got home, changed into her nightgown and immediately got into bed. She was utterly exhausted and almost instantly she fell asleep.

Her phone woke her, playing the rousing music of a popular song. She fumbled on her nightstand to find it and when she did, she saw that it was Nick calling her.

"What's up?" she asked, noticing that it was just after two. A knot formed in her chest. This could only be bad.

"We've got another one," he said curtly.

"Where?"

"She's in the alley behind Madeline's Hair and Nail Spa."

"I'll be right there," she replied. She hung up the phone and shot into action. She dressed quickly and ran a fast brush through her hair, then grabbed her car keys and headed out.

Damn, she'd hoped there wouldn't be another victim, that she and Nick would be able to capture the killer before a fifth woman was murdered.

The only thing she could hope for at this time was with Nick on the job he would find some clues that had been lacking in all the other murders. They needed something to go on, some clue they could run with.

Night still clung to the skies. At least the moon overhead shot down a silvery light that cut through the darkness.

The streets were deserted until she reached the beauty shop. Parked out front was Nick's car, Gravois's vehicle, another patrol car and several other cars she didn't recognize.

She pulled in next to Nick's car and parked, her heart racing with adrenaline. She walked down the side of the shop and turned into the alley.

Several bright lights had been set up and shone on the body and the surrounding area. She nodded to both Nick and Gravois and then gazed down at the victim. Seeing the women in crime scene photos was much different from seeing one of the victims in person.

Her stomach clenched and she fought against nausea as she saw the poor victim. Even though she wore jeans and a bright yellow blouse, it was obvious she'd been stabbed several times in the stomach, but it was her throat and face that sickened Sarah.

The victim's throat was ripped out and her face was shredded beyond recognition. It was gruesome and horrifying to think that another human being could be responsible for this kind of monstrosity.

"We're just waiting for the coroner," Nick said.

She nodded. They couldn't begin their work until after the coroner arrived and examined the body and the conditions. They all turned at the sound of footsteps approaching. Ed Martin came around the corner.

"Gentlemen… Sarah," he said in greeting.

"I thought you understood it was inappropriate for you to be at a crime scene," Nick said, his anger rife in his tone.

"Gravois called me to let me know another murder had occurred and as a businessman in this town I…"

"I don't give a damn who you are, and what I think is it's damned suspicious of you to show up here," Nick replied.

"Suspicious? Do you really think I have something to do with these murders?" Ed asked incredulously.

"Gentlemen, please stop," Gravois said firmly. "Now isn't the time for any arguments."

"Who called this in?" Sarah asked, hoping to further diffuse the situation.

"Zeke did. Apparently, he and his dopehead friend Dwayne Carter decided to come back here and party, but they found her instead," Gravois said. "I've got Zeke locked up in the back of my car and Dwayne is locked up in the back of Brubaker's car. I'm holding them both for questioning."

"Do we know who she is?" Sarah asked.

"Not yet. Hopefully somebody will come forward to help us with an identification," Gravois replied. "We'll take her fingerprints but if she isn't in the system then that won't help us." Gravois then began to take the crime scene photos.

He had just finished up when the coroner, Dr. Douglas Cartwright, arrived with his assistant, Jimmy Leyton. They all remained silent and let Old Man Cartwright do his work.

Cartwright had been the coroner for as long as Sarah remembered. He had to be in his late seventies or early eighties by now, but she'd never heard of him being interested in retiring.

He immediately took the body's temperature and then bagged her hands. Hopefully she'd fought back and gotten some skin from the attacker beneath her fingernails. They could only get so lucky.

She glanced at Nick, who appeared laser-focused on what was going on. Since this was the first murder scene she'd ever been at, she also watched everything that was being done with apt interest.

She so hoped that with this one they could get a good, solid clue as to who the Honey Island Swamp Monster murderer was. So far, their investigation had been just flying by the seat of their pants. Although James Noman was very high on the suspect list, if the blood and bones in his place turned out to be animal, then they would be back to square one. At least if this woman had to die then Sarah hoped her death yielded the clue that broke the case wide open.

Cartwright finally finished and stood up straight. "Jimmy, go get the gurney," he said to his assistant. "Needless to say, I'm ruling this as a homicide," he said. "Manner of death appears to be knife wounds to the stomach. I'd say she's been dead no longer than two hours. I'll know more after conducting the autopsy."

"Can Officer Beauregard and I be at the autopsy?" Nick asked.

"Of course. However, I don't like to put things off so as soon as you are finished up here, come on to the morgue and we'll immediately do the autopsy," Cartwright replied.

Minutes later the body had been taken away and that was when the real police work began. Ryan Staub was called in by Gravois and when he arrived, he went to interview Zeke and Wayne while the other three of them began processing the scene.

They gathered up anything and everything that

had been beneath and around the body. Nick walked between the buildings, hoping to find something on the path the body had been carried in. However, to Sarah's eyes, nothing they collected had anything to do with the murder or murderer. It was mostly just trash.

Almost three hours later they pulled into the morgue's parking lot. The morgue was housed in a small building next to the Black Bayou hospital.

As Sarah got out of her car, a nervous anxiety played in the pit of her stomach. It had been difficult enough to see the Jane Doe dead in person. The autopsy would test her emotional strength in a way she knew it had never been tested before.

Nick joined her at the front of the car. "Are you ready for this?"

"I'm not sure," she replied honestly. "The last time I was here it was to identify the bodies of my parents."

"Oh, Sarah. I'm so sorry," he said. He took a step closer to her and for a brief moment she thought he was going to wrap his arms around her, but he stopped just short of her. "If you want to skip out on this, then I wouldn't have a problem with it."

She smiled up at him. "Thanks, Nick. But I need to do this. I need the experience and I need to hear what her body might tell us."

"Autopsies are pretty brutal. If you need to bow

out at any time while it's going on, don't feel bad about it."

She offered him another smile. "I'll keep that in mind."

Together they entered the building where there was a small reception area with a half a dozen chairs.

A woman Sarah didn't recognize greeted them from behind the window. "Dr. Cartwright is waiting for you. Head straight down the hallway and he's in the last room on the right." She buzzed open the door and Nick and Sarah walked through.

The air was much cooler inside. Sarah fought against a shiver, and she didn't know if it was due to the temperature change or for what was to come. She was definitely dreading this.

They passed two doorways and then came to the last one. Nick knocked on the closed door and Cartwright opened the door to allow them inside. This room also had a small reception room with several chairs, a viewing window and an inner door she knew led into the actual autopsy area.

He handed each of them a plastic suit, a hairnet, and booties and gloves to put on. Once they were all suited up, they went into the room where their Jane Doe was on a steel table. She was covered in a sheet with only her ravaged face showing.

"I would estimate our victim to be between twenty and twenty-five years in age. She weighs one hundred and twenty-seven pounds and is five feet three inches tall," he said.

He took off the sheet that had covered the body, which was now naked. "And now we'll begin."

It was a difficult thing to watch, from the first cut to the last. The room filled with the smell of death and several times Sarah was tempted to bow out.

But she didn't. Cartwright talked into a recorder as he worked, memorializing the surgical process. He finished up with the body, finding a total of four stab wounds in the stomach and an injection site in her arm.

"Her last meal consisted of fish," he said.

"Which she probably ate at home or with friends in the swamp," Nick said.

Dr. Cartwright finally moved to her mouth where he discovered a small piece of blue fabric caught in her bottom teeth. He shut off the recorder as he removed the item and placed it on a sterile table next to him.

"Ladies and gentlemen, we have our first solid clue. It appears she tore this from her attacker's clothes," he said.

Nick moved closer to the table and stared down at the small piece of fabric and then gazed up at her. "We'll have to get it tested, but at first look, it appears that it might have come off a police officer's uniform shirt."

A chill raced up her spine. Was it possible one of

the men she worked with, a man who had taken an oath to protect and serve the people of Black Bayou, was the Honey Island Swamp Monster murderer?

Chapter Six

"I bet the tox screen will come back the same as the others with a high dose of Xanax in her system," Nick said.

"I would hazard a guess that you're right. It's obvious that's how the killer is knocking them out and then carrying them out of the swamp and to the place where he kills them," Cartwright replied.

"Still, I'm really pleased about that little piece of material. At least she got a bite out of him," Nick said. "And we got a nice clue to follow up on."

"Too bad she didn't get any of his skin along with the material," Sarah said.

Nick looked at his partner. He'd seen the play of emotions on her face during the autopsy and there had been several times when he'd thought she was on the verge of dipping out. But she'd hung in there and he was proud of her for it. Autopsies were definitely rough. He knew some seasoned cops who couldn't make it through one.

"Let me put this beneath my microscope and I

can give you a pretty good idea of the blend." Cartwright picked up the small piece of material with his tweezers and placed it beneath a high-powered microscope. "It looks to be about thirty to thirty-five percent cotton and sixty or sixty-five percent polyester." He looked up at them. "That's just my educated guess. I'll send it off to the lab to get it confirmed."

"Then I guess we're finished here," Nick said.

"I uploaded her fingerprints so you can run them through the system and see if you get a hit for an identification."

"Thanks, Dr. Cartwright," Nick replied. He and Sarah took off their protective clothing. As they stepped out of the building, the sun was rising in the sky and painted everything with a soft gold glow.

He heard Sarah's audible sigh of relief. "Are you okay?" he asked.

She flashed that brilliant smile of hers. "I'm fine now that it's over."

"Can I ask you a favor?"

"Sure," she replied.

"Do you mind if I take a look at your shirt label?"

"I don't mind at all." She stepped in front of him, so close he could feel her body heat. The sunlight sparked in her hair and that wonderful floral scent surrounded him.

He was going to have to touch the back of her neck. This was part of the investigation, he told himself. Still, he was reluctant to do this because there was a part of him that wanted to see if her skin was as soft as it looked.

"Nick?"

He realized he'd been standing behind her and doing nothing for too long a time. "Yeah, I'm here," he said and then gently pulled her collar out toward him. He couldn't help that his fingers brushed the skin of her neck.

He quickly looked at the label and then tucked it back in. She turned to gaze at him and her cheeks appeared slightly flushed. "What is it? I've never paid any attention to it before."

He stepped back from her. "It's sixty-five percent polyester and thirty-five percent cotton." Was it really possible a cop was responsible for the murders? Nick wasn't sure what to believe at this point. Noman was still at the top of the suspect list, but this little blue piece of material presented a whole new suspect pool to think about.

"How are you feeling?" he asked. It had already been a long night.

"Energized. Once we get an identification, we'll have a lot more people to interview and hopefully soon we'll have that search warrant in hand." She hesitated a moment and then looked at him somberly. "Nick, surely other people besides police officers wear shirts with the same material makeup."

"Sure," he agreed. "Why don't we head back to the office and see where we need to go from here."

She got into her car and he did the same. There was a sense of urgency inside him, but without an identification of the victim, he couldn't interview her parents or friends.

He was definitely intrigued by the tiny blue piece of fabric that had been found in her teeth. He'd told Sarah that the material could have come from anyone, but he thought it was very possible it had come from an officer's shirt.

How dicey was this going to be? And how dicey was it that he felt such an incredible draw toward his partner? He pulled into the parking lot behind the police station and Sarah parked next to him.

Together they got out of their cars and headed to the door. "I suggest we both get a tall cup of coffee to fuel us for what's probably going to be a very long day," he said.

"At least at this time of the morning the coffee might be decent," she replied.

They went inside and directly to the small break room. Inside the room was a vending machine holding sodas and snacks, a round table, and a small table holding a coffee maker. Thankfully the coffee carafe was nearly full and the brew smelled nice and fresh.

They each grabbed one of the foam cups provided and once they had their drinks they headed to their little room. As Sarah took a seat, he set his coffee down and then went to the whiteboard, where he added Jane Doe to their list of victims.

"We need to get Staub's and Brubaker's interviews of Zeke and Dwayne," he said.

"Their reports should be done now and they should be at their desks." She got up. "I'll go get them."

She stepped out of the room and he drew a deep breath and stared at the whiteboard. So much carnage done by a man...no, it was definitely a monster. It would take a monster to do what had been done to those women.

How did he move so well under the radar? How could he commit these murders and not leave anything of himself behind? Most serial killers began to make mistakes, but not this guy. Five dead and the killer didn't appear to be getting sloppy or disorganized. He had to be incredibly intelligent.

But somehow the latest victim had gotten a bite of a shirt. He hoped like hell that little blue piece of material led them to the killer.

"Sorry it took so long," Sarah said as she came back through the door a few minutes later. "Ryan was still typing up his notes, but I've got them both now."

She laid the papers on the table and he sat to go over them. She moved her chair closer to him so she could review them with him.

The interview was much like the one they had conducted with Zeke, and Dwayne's mirrored Zeke's. The two had just been hanging around and had accidentally stumbled on the body.

Nick looked at Sarah in frustration. “I just find it a huge coincidence that these two men have somehow bumbled their way into being around two of the bodies.”

“Do you think maybe our killer is two people?” she asked.

Nick considered the question thoughtfully. “No, I believe we’re looking for one man. And to be honest, I can’t imagine Zeke and Dwayne carrying out these kinds of murders while drugged up or sober. I just don’t think they’re smart or organized enough.”

“I just wonder what they might have seen or heard while they were out on the streets, something that they haven’t told us, something they don’t even know is important,” she replied.

“Who knows,” he replied. “All I know for sure is our killer is definitely organized and smart. He’s managed to commit these murders without leaving anything behind…no foot or fingerprints…nothing.”

“But now we have a little piece of material,” she said with obvious hope in her tone.

“She must have fought hard for her life, and now we need to fight just as hard to find this killer for her.”

Sarah was silent for several minutes and then released a deep sigh. She looked toward the room’s closed door and then leaned closer to him, so close he could see tiny shards of silver in the depths of her bright blue eyes.

"I keep wondering, who would make those girls feel safe enough to walk out of the swamp with him? And who would have the knowledge to pull off a crime like this and leave absolutely no forensic evidence behind?" Her voice was just a mere whisper.

"A cop," he replied, his voice also a whisper.

"Bingo." She sat back in her chair and her eyes grew dark. "Although I find it very hard to believe that a man I've worked with for years, a man I might have been friends with for years, could be our monster."

"At this point, all we can do is follow the evidence," he replied.

A knock sounded on the door and then it opened. It was Ryan. "Hey, we got a hit on her fingerprints," he said. "Her name is Kristen Ladouix. She was arrested twice for having drug paraphernalia on a public street. I pulled her rap sheet and all the information available on her and printed it off for you." He handed Nick the sheets of paper.

"Thanks, man," Nick replied. Ryan left the room and Nick got up to change the Jane Doe on the whiteboard to Kristen Ladouix.

He returned to his chair and looked at what Ryan had brought him. "She was twenty-four years old and it looks like her parents live here in town. Grab your coffee and let's go."

They stepped back outside where the sun was bright and warm. "Your car or mine?" she asked.

"Mine," he replied.

They took off and headed toward the address given for Kristen's parents. For the next four hours they interviewed not only Kristen's parents but also several of her friends.

They learned that Kristen drifted from house to house in the swamp. She had no boyfriend and she was battling her drug addiction, which meant both Zeke and Dwayne probably knew her.

It was just after five o'clock when they finally called it quits for the day. Given the fact that their day had started at two in the morning, Nick was exhausted and he knew Sarah was, too.

"We'll regroup in the morning," he said as she closed down her computer. "Same place…same time."

"I'll be here," she replied. She smiled at him but her smile wasn't quite as big as usual.

"It's been a long day," he said as they walked out together. He was impressed that she hadn't complained once throughout the day.

"It's been a hell of a long day," she replied. "But at least we're making progress. I'm just sorry we didn't hear anything on our search warrant. I hope Judge Epstein isn't out of town."

"Hopefully we'll hear something on it tomorrow." He walked with her to her car door.

Why was it that every time he told her goodbye, he fought the need to pull her into his arms and kiss her? And why was it she looked at him as if she wanted his kiss? Or was he only imagining that?

There was an awkward silence between them for several moments. "I'll just see you in the morning," she finally said, and quickly slid into her car.

He watched as she drove away and then he got into his car. God, he was exhausted, but that didn't explain his growing feelings for Sarah.

He liked her. He liked her a lot. She was bright and had a sharp sense of humor that matched his own. Even though they were working together, he enjoyed his time spent with her. When they were just resting for a moment their conversations about other things came easily.

Still, he was afraid to make any kind of a move on her because if it all went wrong it could potentially make their working relationship very difficult, and that's the last thing he wanted to happen.

He was so tired he decided to skip dinner and just head straight up to bed. Even then it took him a while to fall asleep as his brain churned with visions of the murder victims, the interviews they had conducted that day and the possibility that the little piece of blue fabric had come from a police officer's uniform.

He must have finally drifted off to sleep, for he awakened suddenly with fight-or-flight adrenaline flooding through his veins. He bolted upright, grabbed his gun from his nightstand and then quickly turned on the lamp.

It illuminated the room in a soft glow. Nothing. There was nobody. There was absolutely nothing in the room to warrant his explosive reaction. He drew in a couple of deep breaths and slowly relaxed. It must have been a dream that had jerked him out of his sleep.

He placed his gun back on his nightstand, turned off the lamp and settled back in. Then he heard it…a strange rattling noise coming from under his bed. In fact, there was more than one rattling sound.

What the hell?

He turned the lamp on once again and then grabbed his phone and turned on the flashlight feature. He bent over and looked beneath his bed. He froze as his blood ran cold.

Snakes…rattlesnakes. They coiled and churned together in a mass of deadliness.

SARAH'S PHONE AWAKENED HER. It was just after two in the morning and as she grabbed the phone, she stifled a groan. Surely there couldn't be another body already.

The caller ID read Brubaker. She frowned. Why would Ian be calling her at this time of the night? "Ian?" she answered.

"Hey, Sarah, I thought you might want to know that I just took a call from your partner. Apparently, he's trapped in his room at Irene's because there's a bunch of rattlesnakes under his bed."

"What?" She bolted upright. Rattlesnakes under his bed? Icy chills rushed through her body. Was she having some sort of a nightmare? How could this even be real?

"Uh… Sarah, are you there?"

"Yeah, thanks, Ian," she replied.

She disconnected quickly and dressed as fast as she could in a pair of jeans and a T-shirt that had a Black Bayou Police Department logo on the front. She buckled on her holster, grabbed her gun and then flew out of her house.

Rattlesnakes under his bed? How on earth had something like that even happened? Had he been bitten? God, if he didn't get the antivenin in time, he could potentially die. What paramedic would be willing to get him out of a room full of poisonous snakes?

Her head spun with all kinds of bad scenarios as fear tightened her chest and made it difficult to breathe. The back of her throat closed off after she released a gasp of fear.

She couldn't lose Nick. The whole town needed him. She needed him. Oh God, who could have done such a heinous thing as to put snakes in his room? How had something like that even been accomplished?

The streets were dark until she turned down the

street where Irene Tompkin's house was located. There she saw the swirling red and blue lights of Gravois's vehicle and another patrol car. She pulled up along the curb, as Nick's car and another one was in the driveway.

She jumped out of her car and ran toward the front door, her heart banging an anxious rhythm in her chest. The first person she saw in the entryway was Nick.

He was clad only in a pair of black boxers. Seeing him alive and seemingly okay caused a burst of deep emotion to explode inside her. She ran to him and leaped into his arms, sobs of relief coursing through her.

"Sarah, it's okay," he said softly. "I'm all right."

She looked up at him. "Oh, Nick, I was so scared for you."

She barely got the words out of her mouth when his lips suddenly took hers. It was a fiery kiss that instantly sliced through her fear with steaming desire.

It was as quick as it was hot. He instantly drew back from her. "I'm sorry, Sarah…that…that shouldn't have happened."

"I… I've wanted it to happen," she replied.

At that moment heavy footsteps came down the staircase. Gravois came into view as he walked down to where they stood. He was followed by Colby Shanks. Gravois looked both tired and angry. "Gator bagged five so far and he's got a couple more left to get."

"How did this even happen? H-how on earth did they get in Nick's room?" Sarah asked. This was only one of the many questions she had among others. Gravois looked pointedly at Nick.

She glanced at Nick and tried to focus on what he might say instead of how very hot he looked clad just in his underwear. His body was amazing. His shoulders were so broad and his hips were slim. His arms were well-muscled, as were his long legs. She hadn't even had the time to process the very quick, very good kiss they had just shared.

"I made a very big mistake when I moved into the room," Nick said and a muscle ticked in his jaw. "I didn't check to see if the back door was locked or not. It was a stupid mistake that could have been a deadly error."

He raked a hand through his dark hair. "I didn't think that old fire escape would actually hold anyone, but it must because somebody must have sneaked up those stairs while I was sleeping and put those snakes in my room." His eyes were darker than she'd ever seen them. "Thank God I heard their rattles before I stepped a foot out of bed."

"As soon as I got the call, I sent Officer Lynons to the swamp to get hold of Gator, who is up there now getting all the snakes into a bag," Gravois said. Officer Judd Lynons was a thirty-five-year-old man who had spent the first ten years or so of his life in the swamp.

"Once Gator has all of them wrangled, we'll go in and fingerprint the door and the fire escape. Hopefully we can lift a couple of prints that will give us the identity of who is responsible for this," Gravois said.

"This was attempted murder," Sarah said, once again fighting a chill that tried to race up her spine.

"That's what it appears to be and we'll investigate it as such," Gravois replied. "It was definitely a devious way to try to hurt Nick."

"Where is Nene?" Sarah asked, suddenly thinking about the older woman. She must have been terrified to wake up to the news that there were rattlesnakes in her home.

"She's in the kitchen with Ralph, her other boarder," Nick explained.

"Is she okay?"

"She's surprisingly fine," Nick replied. "She seems to be taking it all very well."

"She's a strong woman," Gravois said.

Gator came down the stairs with Judd following behind him. Gator carried over his shoulder a large burlap bag that writhed with movement. He also had a pair of jeans and a T-shirt which he tossed to Nick. "Thought you might need these," he said.

"Thanks," Nick replied. "So, what was the grand total?" He gestured to the bag.

"Eight big ones," Gator replied. "I'd say somebody doesn't like you too much, Mr. Nick."

"Yeah, I got the message loud and clear," Nick replied. "If you all will excuse me for just a minute, I'll just get dressed."

He walked over to a doorway that she assumed led to a guest bathroom and closed the door behind him. It was a shame for him to cover up his hunky body. And that kiss, it had momentarily taken her breath away. She was just disappointed it hadn't lasted longer. She had a feeling they would definitely need to talk about it later.

"We checked out the entire upstairs, but the snakes were confined to Nick's room," Judd said.

"If Mr. Judd would take me back home now, I'll release these snakes back into the wild," Gator said.

Nick came back into the room, now clad in the jeans and a gray T-shirt. Gravois said, "Judd, go ahead and take Gator home. Shanks and I will go back up there and start processing the scene. Nick, as the victim in all this, you realize you can't be part of the investigation. This is going to take us a while."

"Nick, you want to come to my place to hang out until this is all squared away?" Sarah asked, hoping her invitation sounded casual.

"That's a good idea, Nick. We're still going to be a couple of hours here," Gravois said.

Nick looked at Sarah. "Are you sure you don't

mind? You could just go home now and go back to bed."

"I'm far too wired up to go back to sleep and no, I don't mind at all, otherwise I wouldn't have offered," she replied.

Nick frowned. "My car keys are upstairs."

"That's okay. I'll drive you," Sarah replied. She turned to Gravois. "Is there anything else you need from him?"

"Not at this moment, but I'll need to get an official statement from you, Nick," Gravois replied. "But that's something we can get to later. You're free to go now. I'll just check in with both of you sometime tomorrow."

Nick and Sarah left the house. "What in the hell, Nick," she said once they were in her car.

"Imagine my surprise when I heard the rattling beneath the bed and then saw those snakes," he replied.

"I can't imagine any of it. Just thinking about it sends shivers up and down my spine," she said. "I can't imagine who would do something so vile, so cunning as that." Despite the fact that it was the middle of the night, she still smelled the faint scent of his cologne wafting from him.

"My first question to you would be who have you fought with or had a bad time with in town? Who might hold a grudge against you? But I know you haven't had much of a chance to interact with anyone other than in the investigation," she said.

"You've got that right," he replied. "The only thing I can think of off the top of my head is that we've now somehow officially threatened somebody with our investigation."

She pulled into her driveway and parked and then they both got out of the car. They were silent as she unlocked the door and they went inside. "How about a drink?" she asked. "I've got whiskey and rum. I can't think of a better reason to have one than snakes under your bed."

He released a small, tight laugh. "You're right, and I'd love a whiskey and cola." He sank down on the sofa.

"Coming right up." She went into the kitchen and made the drink for him and then one for herself. She carried them both into the living room, set them on the coffee table and then she collapsed onto the sofa next to him.

"So, what do you think has threatened who?" she asked. She definitely wanted to discuss this, but at some point before she took him home, she intended to talk about the explosive kiss they had shared for far too brief a time.

"Really the only thing I can think of is that little piece of blue material threatened somebody."

"But who would know about that except for us?" She watched as he took a drink before replying.

"Gravois would have known," he replied.

"Surely you don't believe he's our monster," she replied in protest. "There's no way I believe he has anything to do with those murders. I know Gravois and there's absolutely no way."

"But he probably told somebody in the department about the evidence we got and I would guess by noon today almost all of the officers in the department knew about it."

It was her turn to take a big gulp of her drink. "Then you really believe one of the officers is our main suspect." Even the warm burn of the whiskey couldn't take away the chill of thinking that one of her workmates was the monster they sought.

"At this point in time I believe it's more possible than not. Got any idea who might like to wrangle snakes in their spare time?"

"I wouldn't have a clue," she replied. "Although Judd Lynons has a little experience in the swamp, I think it has to be somebody who is well acquainted with it." She took another drink and then placed her hand on Nick's knee.

"Oh, Nick, when I think of what might have happened if you'd been unaware and had stepped out of your bed for anything, it makes me sick to my stomach. You could have been bitten dozens of times. You could have died or at the very least become very, very sick."

His hand covered hers. "Trust me, I'm well aware of that."

"How did you manage to get off the bed with the snakes still in the room?" She tried to fight against the delicious warmth that flooded through her at his touch.

A dry laugh escaped him. "Very carefully. Actually, Gator distracted the creatures under my bed while I made my escape into the hallway. By the way, how did you even know about all this?"

"Ian called me after getting the call from you," she explained. "He thought I might want to know what was happening to my partner."

As they continued to discuss the night's events and the potential suspect pool, they imbibed in another drink and she found herself seated closer to him on the sofa.

She wasn't sure who leaned in first, but suddenly his lips were on hers in a tender kiss that deepened as he dipped his tongue in to taste hers.

The kiss grew less tender and more hungry. His arms pulled her tighter against him. She wrapped hers around his neck, wanting to get closer…closer still to him. She felt as if she'd wanted his kiss for months…for years and now she couldn't get enough of him.

Their tongues battled together and the kiss continued until she was utterly breathless. His lips left hers and instead trailed nipping kisses down the length of her throat.

His hands moved to cup her breasts and she moaned with pleasure. However, her moan seemed to snap whatever had gripped him. He pulled his hands away from her and then he stopped kissing her.

He stared at her with dark eyes that still held a hunger that fired through her blood. "Sarah, I'm so sorry." He swiped a hand through his hair and released a deep sigh. "I… I can't seem to help myself around you."

"Please don't apologize," she replied, her heart still thundering an accelerated beat in her chest.

"It's obvious I have a very strong physical attraction to you…"

"As I have for you," she interjected.

"But, Sarah, we can't do this. We need to maintain a professional relationship."

"Why can't we have both?" She leaned closer to him. "I'm not looking for forever, Nick. I'm aware that once we solve this crime you'll go back to New Orleans. I just want you, Nick, and it won't change the way we work together."

"Sarah, you're killing me here," he whispered softly.

She got to her feet, her heart still beating a chaotic rhythm as warmth suffused her body. "Instead of me taking you home, why don't you let me take you to my bedroom."

She had never been so forward in her entire life, but she had never felt this kind of desire for a man before. It was raw and rich and surely if they made love just once it would get it out of their systems. She held her hand out to him.

Chapter Seven

Nick felt as if he'd been drugged by his desire for her. At some place in the very back of his mind, he knew this was all a bad idea, but kissing Sarah had flooded his veins with the desire for more, for so very much more. Her hand beckoned him to have more and he couldn't deny his own hunger for her.

He slid his hand over hers and stood and allowed her to lead him down the hallway. He followed her past a bedroom that appeared to be a guest room and on the other side was an office. She turned to the left and into her bedroom.

The room smelled of her, the evocative scent that further dizzied his head. The king-size bed was rumpled, with a spread in bright pink and white yanked back to expose pale pink sheets. A silver lamp created a pool of soft light.

It was obvious she had jumped out of bed and run when she'd heard about the snakes in his room. He was sorry she'd been so frightened for him, but right now all he could think about was how much he wanted her.

He immediately drew her back into his arms and captured her lush lips once again with his. She tasted of a little bit of whiskey and a whole lot of hot passion.

He pulled her closer and she molded her small body to his. He loved how she fit so neatly against him…like their bodies had specifically been made for each other.

The kiss continued until they were both breathless. She finally stepped back from him and swept her T-shirt over her head. She wore a plain white bra and he'd never seen anything that looked sexier. Until she took off the bra.

Her breasts were fairly small and absolute perfection. Her nipples were erect and he wanted nothing more than to taste them. His knees weakened and threatened to buckle with the sweet, hot desire that shot through him.

"Are you sure about this, Sarah?" he asked, wanting to give her an out if she needed one. "I want you to be very sure about this."

"I'm completely sure. I want you, Nick," she replied, her voice husky. "I… I feel like I've wanted you for a very long time."

He yanked his shirt over his head, all caution thrown to the wind. They were two intelligent adults. Surely they could enjoy this night together without letting it interfere with their day-to-day working relationship.

This thought erased the last of his worries and instead unleashed the desire he'd had for Sarah since the first day she'd smiled at him.

They finished undressing until she was just in her panties and he was in his boxers. Together they got into the bed and he pulled her back into his arms.

Her bare breasts against his chest felt warm and right as his mouth plied hers with all the fire that burned inside him. She answered him with a fire of her own as her tongue brushed against his and her hands clutched at his back.

As he began to trail kisses down her throat, he slowly rolled her over on her back. His mouth continued down until he captured one of her nipples.

He licked and sucked, loving the sound of her sweet moans. He licked at the first one and then the other. His blood surged inside him and he was fully aroused.

However, he wasn't ready to take her yet. He wanted to pleasure her as much as possible before that happened. His hand slid from her breast down the flat of her stomach and then back and forth across the top of her panties. She arched her hips and moaned in obvious frustration.

Then he slid his fingers over the top of her panties to the place where she wanted him most. She gasped and moved her hips against him and then stopped and wiggled her panties down to her feet. She kicked them off and then he caressed her again.

This time he felt her damp warmth and the rising tension inside her. He teased her at first, dancing his fingers against her in a light flutter, and then he moved his fingers faster and faster. He felt her release as she shuddered against him and cried out his name. Her climax shot his desire for her even higher.

He kicked his boxers off, his need for her now all-consuming. But before he could take her, her hand encircled him. "Ah, Sarah," he groaned as her hand slid up and down the turgid length of him.

He allowed it for only a moment or two and then pushed her hand away and moved between her legs. He hovered above her for only a moment and then moaned with sheer pleasure as he entered her. She wrapped her legs around his back, pulling him deeper inside her.

He locked gazes with her as he began to pump his hips. Her eyes shone with a wild desire. Slowly at first, he slid in and out of her. Her eyes closed as she hissed a soft "yes" and her hands clung to either side of his hips.

His pace increased as the pressure inside him built. Faster and faster, he moved. She had another orgasm and at the same time he climaxed as well.

He finally rolled over to the side of her, his breaths coming in deep gasps that mirrored hers. They remained that way for several long minutes, until their breathing had returned to some semblance of normal.

She placed her hand on his chest and rose up a bit and smiled at him. "That was way better than I'd imagined."

He grinned. "Have you been imagining this for a long time?"

"Only since the very first day you walked into the office," she replied.

"I started imagining this the first time you smiled at me," he confessed. "But you realize this wasn't the right thing for us to do."

"How could something that felt so right be so wrong?" she replied. "Nick, this doesn't have to interfere at all with our working together. We are two rational adults and we can handle this, right?"

Her blue eyes were so appealing and she was so earnest. "I hope so," he finally replied.

"Now, since it's so late, why don't you just spend the rest of your night here."

It felt ridiculous for him to insist she take him home. It was just after four in the morning and neither of them would be any good unless they got some sleep.

"Okay. Why don't we sleep until about noon and then head into the office."

"Sounds good to me. I'll be right back," she replied as she got out of the bed. "Feel free to use the guest bathroom in the hallway before we go to sleep."

As she disappeared into her bathroom and closed the door, he got up and grabbed his boxers from the floor. He went into the bathroom across the hall, cleaned up and put his boxers back on.

He stared at his reflection in the mirror above the sink. Damn, everything had happened so fast there hadn't been a single thought about birth control. It had been over three years since he'd last had sex. Was that what had made making love to Sarah so amazing? Because it had been utterly amazing.

He sluiced cold water over his face, suddenly exhausted. There was a lot to process…snakes in his room and the possibility that a cop was their killer, but he couldn't think about all that tonight. He definitely couldn't think about the fact that he'd just made love to his partner.

After some sleep he would better be able to handle all the new developments and emotions. He left the bathroom and returned to the bedroom where she was back in the bed and clad in a bright pink spaghetti-strap nightgown. She looked positively charming with the pink of the gown and her hair tousled in disarray.

He slid into the bed and she immediately moved to his side, obviously wanting to cuddle as they fell asleep. He'd almost forgotten that he'd once been a snuggler, too, so he had no problem with her filling his arms.

"Good night, Nick," she said softly, her voice already drowsy with impending sleep.

"Night, Sarah," he replied. The lamp on the nightstand was still on, but it didn't deter either of them from finding sleep.

Nick awakened first. The sun shone bright through the blinds at the bedroom windows, letting him know it was probably time for them both to wake up.

However, he was reluctant to move out of the bed. His body was spooned around hers and she fit neatly against him. She felt small and fragile and he realized even though he hadn't known her for very long, he had developed real, deep feelings for her, feelings that went far beyond their partnership in crime.

But their relationship couldn't go anywhere. He had nothing to offer her for any kind of future. His ex-wife had told him he was a terrible husband, and so he would never try to be a husband again. Why make another woman miserable?

The fact that he was even thinking these thoughts after only one night with Sarah disturbed him. It was definitely time to get up and get to work.

He rolled away from her and she immediately woke. She stretched like a kitten waking up from a nap and offered him a groggy smile. "Good morning…or is it afternoon?"

"It's eleven thirty," he replied as he pulled his T-shirt over his head and then reached for his jeans. At the same time, she slid out of the bed.

"Give me about twenty minutes and I'll be ready to go." She walked over to her closet and grabbed a uniform and then headed to the bathroom.

"I'll be in the living room," he replied. He left her bedroom and sank down on the sofa to wait for her. His head whirled with myriad thoughts that would take time to sort out.

True to her word, about twenty minutes later she walked into the living room, looking and smelling fresh from her shower.

"When we get to my place you can just drop me off and I'll meet you at the station within a half an hour or so," he said as they got in her car.

"Aren't you afraid to go back into that room?" she asked.

"Nah, I have faith that Gator got all the snakes out. Now all we have to do is try to figure out is what snake put them all in my room," he replied darkly.

SARAH SAT IN the small room in the station and stared at the whiteboard. She should be thinking about all the criminal activity that had taken place recently, but all she could think about at the moment was the night she'd shared with Nick.

Making love with him had been magical. He'd

been both tender and masterful, taking her to heights of pleasure she'd never known before.

Almost as magical had been falling asleep in his arms. She'd felt so safe in his embrace as she'd drifted off to sleep. His arms had felt big and strong as they'd enfolded her and his familiar scent had enveloped her.

She knew she shouldn't be developing any real feelings for him, but she couldn't rein in her heart. The truth was she was more than half crazy about him.

She admired his professionalism. He challenged her to think deeper, to analyze everything. More than that, he made her feel like a breathless teenager when she was around him. She didn't remember feeling this way about her ex-fiancé and at the time she'd believed she had loved him with all her heart. But things felt different with Nick.

And who had tried to kill him last night? It had been a particularly cunning way to try to commit murder. One step off his bed and he could have been bitten dozens of times.

Again, chills raced up and down her spine at the very thought. Thank God he'd heard the rattles before he'd made a move. Who could have gotten those snakes from the swamp, carried them up that old fire escape and then released them into Nick's room?

She jerked around as the door flew open. She stifled a groan as Ryan walked in. "Good morning,

Short-Stuff," he said as he threw himself into the chair next to her.

"What do you want, Ryan?" she asked, unable to keep her irritation out of her voice.

He gave her a hurt expression. "Gee, I never get a chance to talk to you anymore. You and Mr. Hot Stuff are always together."

"We're working," she replied pointedly.

"I think you're doing more than that together. I see the way you look at him. You've got the hots for him."

"Don't be ridiculous. I look at him like he's my partner and my friend." The last thing she would want was for her and Nick to become the subject of office gossip. The last thing she wanted was for anything to undermine her professionalism to her coworkers. Nobody had to know what was going on between her and Nick. It was their private, personal business.

"What have you two come up with so far? You have a suspect in mind?"

"We don't have anyone in particular, but we're definitely narrowing it down," she said, careful to not give anything away.

"I heard you got a nice piece of evidence from the last victim," he replied.

"I guess news travels fast around here," she replied.

"But it's a big deal," he said. "We got nothing from

all the other victims. At least you now have something to work with," he said.

"Yeah, we'll just have to see where the evidence takes us," she replied.

Before she could say anything else, the door opened and Nick walked in. Ryan immediately jumped up out of the chair and smiled at Nick. "Hey, man, I was just visiting a little bit with Sarah."

"No problem," Nick replied.

"I just haven't had a chance to talk to her lately. But I'll just get out of here now and let you two do your thing."

He didn't wait for Nick to say anything, as he quickly left the room. Nick sat in the chair opposite her and grinned with amusement. "Anything important come up in your conversation with him?"

She smiled. "There's never anything important in my conversations with him, although he did ask about where we were at in the investigation. I didn't tell him anything other than we were narrowing down on suspects."

As usual, Nick smelled fresh and clean and of the spicy cologne she found so attractive. He was clad in navy slacks and a light blue shirt and as always, her heart beat a little faster at the mere sight of him.

"Uh...before we get down to work, I think we need to talk for a minute about last night."

Her heart seemed to stop beating as she stared at

him. "Please don't take it back. Nick, please don't tell me you regret it," she replied softly.

He smiled, that soft smile of his that warmed her heart like a fiery furnace. "How could I take back something that was so wonderful?"

She continued to breathe again. "It was wonderful. So what do we need to talk about?"

"I wanted you to know that it has been years since I've been with anyone, but things happened so fast last night I didn't think about birth control."

"It's also been years for me," she admitted. "And I'm on the pill, so we're safe." It was a slightly awkward conversation and she felt the faint blush that warned her cheeks. She supposed these kinds of conversations happened a lot in the dating world today, although she had to remind herself that they were definitely not dating.

All they'd shared was a very hot night together, one that she'd be eager to repeat again and again. However, the ball was in his court on that issue.

"So, let's talk about last night and what happened in my room," he said. "Let's talk about the fact that I was a damned fool not to check to make sure the back door in my room wasn't locked." He grimaced. "I only looked at it once on the day that I moved in and I guess in my mind once I saw the terrible condition of the fire escape, I dismissed the idea of anyone coming in that way. It was a very stupid mistake on my part."

"Don't beat yourself up, Nick. Who would have guessed somebody would use those stairs to dump nearly a dozen snakes in your room?" she replied.

"I spoke to Gravois on my way in. They didn't get any prints off the door or the railing," he said. "I didn't think they would. Whoever did this was smart…smart enough not to leave any prints behind."

A tight pressure built up in her chest. "Do you think it was our killer?"

"I believe it was definitely somebody who wanted to take me out of the investigation," he replied, his eyes the color of stormy skies. "So yeah, I think it was our killer."

"Why didn't he just burst in and try to kill you?"

"Probably he didn't because he knew I'd have a gun within my reach," he replied.

She opened up her computer and turned it on. "If we believe a cop is behind this, then maybe I should pull up the schedules for this week, especially for the night of this last murder. At least it will show us who was on duty both that night and last night and we can eliminate them from our suspect pool," she said.

"It's a good place to start," he agreed.

"Wait…there's a notification that I have a message waiting." She clicked on the message and then looked up at him in excitement. "We just got our search warrant for James Noman's place."

"There's a lot of blood in that shanty, and I imagine living in the swamp he would be quite adept at snake-handling, so let's go."

She printed the search warrant off using the printer in the little office area down the hall and then together they took off in Nick's car.

She didn't know how the fabric caught in Jane Doe's teeth might relate to James Noman, but Nick was definitely right about the blood in his shanty and the fact that the man probably knew all about snakes.

Even though solving these murders would mean the end of Nick's time here, more than anything she wanted this vicious killer off the streets and behind bars.

ADRENALINE PUMPED THROUGH Nick as he parked in Vincent's lot. At the moment James Noman was as much a suspect as anyone. He would have access to the women who lived in the swamp, although he had no idea if the man had a vehicle or not to transport the bodies into town.

However, James could probably move like a shadow on the streets, getting in and out of the dump of the women without being seen by anyone, and there was no question in Nick's mind that the man was capable of catching snakes.

In the back of his mind, Nick still held the possibility of the killer being a cop, but right now he had Noman in his sights and he couldn't wait to explore that shanty in greater detail.

He had to stay focused on solving this crime as soon as possible. He needed to get away from Sarah as quickly as possible, before things between them got too deep. He'd already developed feelings for her he'd never expected to happen. The last thing he wanted to do was hurt her in any way.

As always, as they entered the swamp, his heart beat faster and he fought against the dark memories of his childhood trauma that sometimes haunted his dreams in the form of nightmares.

He thought it would get easier, but each time he had to enter the marshlands, his anxiety went through the ceiling. His throat threatened to close off and his mouth became unusually dry. The last thing he wanted was for Sarah to see his anxiousness. He didn't want her to realize that the big, bad homicide cop was nothing more than a ball of nervous angst.

Even now he was acutely aware of her as they moved through the swamp. Despite the pungent odors surrounding him, he could still smell the scent of her perfume. He imagined he could feel her body heat even though she trailed behind him by several feet.

He clutched his evidence kit harder in an attempt to stay focused on the matter at hand. He intended to take samples of the blood and take photos of all the bones on the walls. He was hoping Dr. Cartwright would be able to give them some quick answers without him having to send it all to a lab where it would take weeks or even months to get results back.

If the blood came back as human, then a lot more would have to be done to process what all was there and he would probably need to call in more officers to help.

As the trail narrowed, he turned around to face his partner. "Are you okay?" She nodded in response.

He turned back around and continued walking, trying to make as little noise was possible as they got closer to Noman's shanty. He'd definitely like to find the man at home and be able to question him.

They finally reached the bridge that led to Noman's shanty. He paused at the foot of it and looked all around. Like last time they'd been here, the place appeared deserted from the outside.

His heart raced fast in his chest. They had no idea if Noman had a gun or not. There was no way to even know if he was inside the structure.

"Mr. Noman," he yelled, and waited for a reply. When there was none, he shouted one more time and then carefully maneuvered over the rickety bridge. Once he was on the other side, he drew his gun and watched as Sarah came across.

When they were together on the porch, he immediately went to the broken window and looked inside. There was nobody there. He holstered his gun and went to the front door. It easily opened and the two of them stepped inside.

The stench inside was horrendous and the place looked just like it had before. He glanced at the old quilt on the cot. It was multicolored and had shades of blue in it. Was that where the blue fabric that had been in Jane Doe's mouth had come from? Perhaps he had wrapped the victim up in the quilt before he'd killed her or as he'd carried her out of the swamp.

"Why don't you take the photos of the bones and I'll get busy taking some blood samples," he said.

"Sounds like a plan," she agreed. "The sooner we get out of here the better as far as I'm concerned. This place definitely creeps me out."

It creeped him out as well. As she began snapping photos, he got busy scraping off blood samples from various places in the large pool of dried blood and storing them in his evidence kit.

They were just about finished when the door flew open and James Noman came inside. "Who are you people and why are you in my home?" he asked, with anger flaring his nostrils and a definite edge in his deep tone.

Nick slowly rose from where he'd been crouched down and Sarah inched closer to his side. James Noman was rail thin with dark hair that spilled down past his shoulders. He wore only a pair of nasty-looking gray shorts and his eyes were dark and wild.

He also brought with him a sick energy that instantly put Nick on edge. "Mr. Noman, I'm Nick Cain and this is my partner, Sarah Beauregard," he replied in a soft, hopefully calming voice. "We're here with a search warrant to take some samples of this blood. We're almost finished here and then we'll leave." Nick attempted to hand him the search warrant, but James waved it away.

"Mr. Noman, can I ask you a few questions?" Sarah asked, and gave him her brightest smile.

He stared at her for a long moment. "You're real pretty. I never get any pretty girls here."

"Thank you, so can I ask you a few things?" Sarah kept her tone light and easy.

He slowly nodded. "Okay. Only you, not him." He pointed to Nick with a frown.

"Is James Noman your real name?" she asked.

He frowned. "I don't know my real name. I picked James and then decided to call myself Noman because I am no man to anyone. I've been alone here for as long as I can remember."

"What happened to your parents?" she asked curiously.

"I don't know. I don't remember them," he replied.

"I'm sorry to hear that, James. So, you've always been alone here?" Her voice held a touch of sympathy. While she continued to ask him questions, Nick returned to collecting the last of the blood samples.

"Why are you here? Why is he doing that?" James asked, a thick tension back in his voice as he divided his gaze between her and Nick.

"Have you heard about the swamp women who have been murdered?" she asked.

He frowned. "No, but nobody ever talks to me. People don't much like me and I don't much like people. I talk to the trees and the plants and the animals and that's all I need."

"What are all these bones?" she asked.

"They're the bones of the animals that I've eaten. I put them on the wall to honor them because they gave their lives for me. Sometimes they talk to me, 'specially in the middle of the night."

"And what do they say to you?" she asked.

A smile curved his lips. It wasn't a pleasant smile. "Nothing you need to know." The smile snapped off his face. "So, why are you here? It's not against the law to kill animals for food."

Nick joined Sarah's side, having gotten what he needed of the blood samples and feeling a definite shift in James's demeanor and energy. "We're finished in here, Mr. Noman, so we'll just leave now."

"Don't come back. Do you hear me? Don't come back here. It ain't right. It ain't right at all to just walk into a man's home and do stuff," he said, suddenly angrily. "You had no right to come in here."

Nick took Sarah's arm to guide her out the door as James's temper seemed to be growing with each minute that passed. Once they were outside, he had her go over the bridge first and then he quickly followed her.

James stood on his porch, watching them go with narrowed eyes and bunched shoulders. Thank God apparently the man didn't own a gun because Nick wasn't convinced James wouldn't have shot to kill them.

Chapter Eight

The next three days flew by. They continued to interview as many people as possible from any and all the murders. They interviewed family members and friends, all pretty much with the same results.

They'd dropped the blood samples and photos off to Dr. Cartwright, but there had been a deadly car accident on the same day with four dead, so he'd been too busy to get back to them with any results.

It was about seven o'clock in the evening of the third night and they were seated at the table, after having updated their notes.

He leaned back in his chair and released a tired sigh. "You know what I'm thinking about right now?"

She looked up from her computer and smiled at him. As usual that smile of hers tightened all the muscles in his stomach and caused a wave of warmth to sweep over him. "What?" she asked.

"A nice juicy steak and a good, stiff drink."

"Sounds good to me," she replied.

"So, where do two tired cops go to get those things in this town?" he asked.

"The café has a decent steak, but if you want a really good steak and a nice stiff drink, then the place to go is Tremont's."

"Are you up for it?" he asked, and stood.

She immediately jumped up from her chair. "Your car or mine?"

He laughed. "Now that's a woman I don't have to ask twice."

Minutes later they were in his car and headed to the high-end restaurant. "So, are you hungry?" he asked and glanced at her. Even after a ten-hour day, she still looked fresh and pretty.

"I'm starving," she replied.

He focused back on the road, as always fighting his desire for her. Since the last time they'd made love, all he'd been able to think about was being in bed with her once again.

However, he kept telling himself he had to remain strong and not go there again. At least they were spending the rest of this evening out in public because if they were in a private place, he wasn't so sure he could remain so strong.

He pulled up to the sleek-looking restaurant where he had to go around the building to park in the back as the places in front were all full.

He fought the impulse to grab her hand in his as they walked around to the front door. Only then did he touch her and that was by placing his hand on the small of her back as he ushered her inside.

They were greeted by a hostess who led them past a long bar filled with well-dressed drinking men and to a booth toward the back of the busy place. They slid in on either side of the seats with red upholstered bench backs and then the hostess handed each of them a large glossy menu.

"Your server should be with you shortly," she said with a friendly smile and then left their booth.

Both of them immediately began to peruse the menus. "Have you eaten in here often?" he asked.

"Not too often, but occasionally. I can tell you I've never had a bad meal here." She closed the menu and grinned at him. "You made me hungry for a nice, juicy steak."

"Ah, the power of suggestion," he replied with a small laugh. He sobered then. "Before the waitress gets here, let's get one thing straight… I'm paying and I don't want any arguments from you."

"That doesn't mean you aren't going to get one from me." She leaned forward, her eyes sparkling brightly. "We're partners and that means we each pay our own way," she protested.

"But I have an expense account and can ultimately write this off as a business dinner. Besides, Sarah, I really want to pay for your meal tonight. Please let me do that."

She held his gaze for a long moment. “Okay,” she finally relented.

“Good, now that we have that settled, we can move on to other topics of conversation.” At that moment their waitress appeared at their booth.

There were two sizes of the ribeye steak. He got the big one with mashed potatoes and corn and she ordered the smaller size with a baked potato and corn. He ordered a whiskey and Coke and she got an iced tea.

Once their orders were taken and the waitress had scurried away, Nick leaned back in his seat and gazed at Sarah. “Tell me why a pretty, intelligent and charming woman like you isn’t married or have a boyfriend?”

She blushed and averted her gaze from his. “I came really close to getting married about three years ago.”

“So, what happened? Did you get cold feet?”

She looked back at him and released a small, dry laugh. “No. I was all in on it. I was engaged to a man who I adored and we were getting married in three months’ time. I was spending all my time planning the wedding. I got us a venue and we went cake-tasting together and I thought he was all in as well.”

She let go of a deep sigh. “One night we partied with some friends and he got pretty smashed. I put him to bed and as I took his phone out of his pocket, something told me to look at it. I really didn't expect to find anything bad." Her eyes deepened in hue.

"But you did." He fought the desire to reach out and take her hand in his, if nothing else for support as she spoke of what was an obviously hurtful time.

"Oh, I definitely did. I found a recording he'd made of him and one of my best friends having sex and the date stamp on it was for the night before we'd gone to order flowers for the wedding."

Her eyes suddenly snapped with a fiery anger. "The creep was carrying on a full-blown affair with her while planning to marry me. I wasn't sure who I was angrier with, him or the woman who was supposed to be my friend. Anyway, I kicked them both to the curb. Since then, I haven't really been looking for a man to add to my life."

"I'm so sorry that happened to you," he replied. "You deserved so much better than that."

"Thanks, Nick," she replied.

At that moment the waitress arrived with both their drinks and their food. "What about you?" she asked once they had been served and were alone again. "I could certainly ask the same of you. Why isn't a good-looking, intelligent and charming man like you not married or with a girlfriend?"

"Actually, I was married for four years. It's funny, it was about three years ago that like yours, my life fell apart," he said. "My wife sat me down one night and told me I was a lousy husband. I thought everything was fine and that we were trying to start a family and that night she told me she would never have kids with a worthless man like me."

She held his gaze for a long moment. "I can't imagine this, but were you really a lousy husband?" she asked.

"I didn't think I was, but I know through our four-year marriage I was working a lot of hours. According to what she told me, I guess I didn't see her needs. I wasn't available to her the way I should have been so I guess ultimately, I probably was a lousy husband. That's made me realize I should probably never marry again."

"Have you ever considered that maybe she wasn't as patient with you as she should have been? Did she communicate her needs to you? Did she tell you she was unhappy before that night?"

He appreciated that Sarah seemed to be trying to rehabilitate him, but he knew the truth and the truth was he hadn't been and wasn't now great husband material. "No, she really didn't tell me anything until the day she walked out on me."

In fact, she'd never asked him about his work. When he'd tried to talk with her about it, she'd made it clear she wasn't interested in what he did for a living. When he'd ask her how her day had gone, she'd just say okay and that was it.

"Did she work or was she a stay-at-home housewife?" Sarah reached for the bottle of steak sauce on the table.

"Are you really going to do that?" he asked.

"Do what?" she asked.

"Are you really going to smother the goodness of that steak with that stuff?" he asked teasingly.

She laughed. "Yes, I am. I'm a saucy kind of woman." She shook the sauce out in a large pool next to her steak and then put the bottle back where it belonged. "And you never answered my question about your ex."

"She worked as a teller at a bank."

"You realize there's really nobody outside this business that understands the long hours and the dedication it takes in getting bad guys off the streets," Sarah said.

He cut into his steak and nodded in agreement with her. "So your next boyfriend should be another cop. Ryan seems to have a definite thing for you." He'd noticed Staub sniffing around Sarah whenever he got a chance.

"Bite your tongue. That man would be the last one on earth that I would ever want to date," she replied.

Nick was ridiculously happy to hear that even though he shouldn't be. As they ate, they talked about how difficult it was to maintain a relationship with a cop.

"In a perfect world, people in law enforcement should just marry each other," she said. "Except there's nobody in my cop world that I'd want to marry."

"I don't have a cop world anymore," he replied.

"Do you miss being on the police force?" she asked.

"Sure, from time to time I miss it. I mostly miss the companionship of my cop friends. I've tried to stay in touch with them but it's been difficult. Right now, as I told you before, I can work as little or as much as I want. I pick and choose the cases that I work and I don't have to worry about red tape," he replied.

"Don't you eventually want children?" she asked.

"When I married Amy, I wanted two, hopefully a boy and a girl, but now I just don't think about it. What about you? Do you want children?" he asked.

"In a perfect world, if I was happily married, then yes, I'd like to have two kids," she replied. He heard a slightly wistful tone in her voice.

As they continued to eat, they talked about his work and about where she saw herself once this case was solved.

"I'm hoping to gain some respect once this is all over. We have had some crime problems in the past that I would have loved to work and hopefully now Gravois will let me do more than sitting on a corner giving tickets or working the dispatch desk," she said.

"You're too good a cop to be wasted that way," he replied.

Her eyes sparkled as she smiled at him. "Thanks, that means a lot coming from you."

"Well, I mean it," he replied. She had the intelligence and the natural instincts to be a really good cop. All she needed was a chance to show those traits.

"Tell me this, did anything in your entire life scare you more than realizing there were snakes under your bed?" she asked as they continued to eat.

He felt so comfortable with her now. In fact, he felt far closer with her than he had ever felt with his ex-wife. "Actually, that wasn't the scariest time of my life," he slowly admitted. "I told you before that my mother would often take me with her into the swamp. I guess I was about five or six when she took me with her to a client's shanty."

She leaned forward, her gaze intent on his. There were times when he felt as if when they locked gazes it was as powerful a connection as them making love. Her beautiful eyes drew him in so deeply.

"The adult conversation quickly bored me," he continued. "And all I wanted to do was go outside to play, so when nobody was paying any attention to me, I slipped outside and went exploring. It wasn't long before I was completely lost and absolutely terrified."

He released a dry, humorless laugh and looked away from her. "Suddenly the trees looked like tall monsters and I thought the Spanish moss was trying to eat me. I believed there were gators all around me just waiting to grab me with their big jaws and I was absolutely scared to death."

"Ah, poor baby." She reached across the table and took his hand in hers. He looked at her once again and her eyes widened slightly and she squeezed his hand harder. He was sure she could feel the clamminess that had taken over his skin as he'd confessed this fear.

"Oh, Nick, I'm so sorry you had that experience." She finally released his hand but held his gaze intently. "So how hard was it for you to go back into the swamp for this case?"

Feeling her unwavering support, he decided to be completely truthful. "To be perfectly honest, it's been very difficult every time we've had to go in." He laughed. "So much for the big, bad macho homicide cop, right?"

"You're human, Nick, and you had a bad experience as a child. Those kinds of experiences sometimes shape our adult life. But you should have told me about this before now," she replied.

"Why? So you could hold my hand in the swamp?"

"I would hold your hand anytime you needed me to." Her gaze was so soft and so accepting it squeezed his heart tight with a depth of emotion.

"We'd better eat up now before our food gets too cold," he finally said, and swallowed hard against the emotions she evoked in him.

They small-talked for the remainder of the meal. The steak was great and the sides were just as good. As always, their conversation flowed easily and he found himself wondering what it would be like to be married to her.

It was easy for him to imagine coming home from work to her. She would ask him questions about the job he'd done that day. She'd want to know what case he was working on and he'd want to know all about her day and she'd share it all with him.

It was crazy how easily he could imagine it with Sarah and how difficult it had been with Amy. Would it be so different with somebody who shared his same passion? Who loved what he did for a living?

He checked himself. What in the hell was he doing even thinking about being married to Sarah? They were just partners and that was it. He'd be leaving here as soon as the case was solved and he'd go back to his solitary…slightly lonely life in New Orleans.

"Coffee and dessert?" he asked.

"Coffee for sure. I'm not sure about dessert, I'm pretty full," she replied.

"At least look at the dessert menu," he urged her.

"Chocolate lava cake with ice cream and a river of chocolate syrup," she read aloud. "I'm not only tempted, but I'm going for it and you are a very bad influence on my girlish figure."

He laughed. "Stick with me, woman, and I'll lead

you down the path of decadent desserts. And trust me, there is absolutely nothing wrong with your figure."

"Thank you, sir," she replied, and a soft pink filled her cheeks.

He waved for the waitress and ordered the lava cake for her and for himself he got something called the caramel dream, which involved a special spice cake with caramel syrup and butterscotch chips. He got coffee for them both.

Minutes later they had the desserts in front of them. "Hmm, you've got to taste this," he said after taking his first bite. He got a spoonful and held it out toward her.

She leaned forward and took it into her mouth. Just that quickly his desire for her roared back to life. He remembered exactly how her mouth had felt against his and he wanted to taste her again. But the closest he got was when she offered him a spoonful of her lava cake.

An attractive couple appeared by their booth. The man was handsome and well-dressed and the woman with him was absolutely beautiful. "Sarah," he said in greeting.

"Hi, Jackson, hi, Josie," she replied. "Jackson, this is Nick Cain and, Nick, this is Jackson Fortier and his wife, Josie."

The two men shook hands. "We don't intend to interrupt you for long. I just wanted to meet you,

Nick, and let you know you have a lot of people supporting your efforts here."

"Thank you, I appreciate that," Nick replied.

"If you find yourself needing anything at all that you can't get through the department, then feel free to call me and I might be able to help out," Jackson said.

"Again, I appreciate that," Nick said.

"And now we'll just move along and let you enjoy your desserts," Jackson said, and then he and Josie followed the hostess on to their table.

"Jackson is one of the wealthiest men in town and he's a major reason why you are here," Sarah said once the couple was out of ear reach. She then explained to him how Jackson and several of his fellow businessmen had confronted Gravois and demanded he bring in help to solve the murders.

She also shared with him how Jackson, a man from town, had met the lovely Josie from the swamp and the danger Josie had been in when one of Jackson's friends had tried to kill her. Thankfully there had been a happy ending and the bad guy had been arrested.

They were just finishing up their coffee when Nick's phone rang. With a frown he dug it out of his pocket. "It's Dr. Cartwright," he said to Sarah, and then answered the call.

He listened to what the coroner had to tell him, thanked him and then hung up. He gazed at Sarah for a long moment and then released a deep sigh. "All the blood samples from Noman's place came back as animal. There was no human blood and he was able to identify the bones as animal as well."

She frowned as she held his gaze. "So where does that leave us now?"

"With a small piece of blue fabric that is our only clue," he replied.

Her eyes darkened. "And that means our pool of suspects has now narrowed down to the members of the police department."

THE NEXT MORNING Sara arrived early for work. It was a few minutes before seven when she got a cup of coffee and then went to their little workroom.

She set up her computer and then sipped on her coffee. She'd tossed and turned all night as she considered the possibility that one of the men she worked with could be their Honey Island Swamp Monster murderer.

If that wasn't enough it was thoughts of Nick that had kept her from sleep. Even knowing there was no future with him, she found herself falling hard for him.

She'd seen the depth of emotion inside him as he'd talked about being a lousy husband. No matter what had gone down in his marriage, she suspected he'd been hurt deeply.

Even though she hadn't been married to Brent,

they'd dated for three years before he'd betrayed her so badly. She'd not only written Brent out of her life, but also her girlfriend Casey, who had decided it was okay to sleep with Sarah's fiancé. But once her anger had left her, the pain of their betrayal had remained with her. So, just like Nick, she'd been hurt by love before.

Then there was his confession about getting lost in the swamp when he was a little boy and the residual effect it had on his adult life.

She'd wanted to find that lost little boy and comfort him. She'd wanted to gather him into her arms and hold him tightly until he was no longer afraid.

She admired him so much for being able to push through his fear and go into the very heart of the swamp to find a killer. However, it sounded like the next leg of their investigation wouldn't take place in the swamp.

She and Nick had both been through the fires of loss and knowing that had only made her feel closer to him. She had a feeling heartache and betrayal were in her near future. Nick was going to break her heart and if it was true that one of her brothers in the police department was the killer, then she would feel utterly betrayed by that.

She turned as the door opened and was surprised to see Nick, who was also early. "Morning, partner," she said.

He gave her a smile that made her stomach swirl

with warmth. "You're an early bird," he said as he set his cup of coffee on the table.

"I had trouble sleeping last night," she replied.

"Yeah, that makes two of us." He sat across from her. "I imagine we both had the same thoughts keeping us awake."

She seriously doubted he'd lost sleep over her. "The few clues we have point to somebody in the department." She kept her voice low.

"We have the fabric and we also have the fact that all of those women would have trusted a cop who approached them in the swamp." His voice was equally low. "How many officers are there in total?"

"Fourteen, plus Gravois."

He nodded. "First of all, from here on out we write nothing down on the whiteboard. We don't need anyone to walk in here and see what kind of internal investigation we're about to start doing."

"Agreed," she replied.

"We'll document everything on your computer and make sure you take your computer home with you every night."

"Again, agreed," she replied. "So, where do we start?" She dreaded this whole process, but was determined to follow through with it. If the monster was hiding in the department, then he needed to be found.

"We need to pull up the schedules for every officer for as long as they go back."

"That's going to take up most of the day," she replied.

"Then let's go ahead and get started."

For the next four hours or so, Sarah printed off the schedules for all the officers in the past two months, which was all that was available to her online. As she finished with each one, Nick stapled them together and began making a chart of who was where during the nights of the last two murders.

It took them two days to narrow down what they could but there was no way they could know what the officers did on their nights off.

She told him everything she knew about her fellow officers, their personalities and temperaments. They both knew their monster was intelligent and still highly organized. He'd made no mistakes until the last victim, who had gotten that piece of material from someplace on him.

She also told Nick about their living spaces. They were still looking for a killing ground, so they needed to know not only where the officers lived but also if they owned any other property in or just out of town.

On the afternoon of the second day, they went into city hall to research who owned what. By the end of that day, they had more lists to go through and check out.

One of the things Sarah had learned while working with Nick was that a murder investigation wasn't just about chasing a suspect through the swamp or anywhere else. Good police work was also long hours of research and desk time.

So far, they had managed to keep their investigation close to their chests. However, sooner rather than later they were going to have to start interrogating the cops in the department, and that was going to open up a whole new can of worms.

It was just after seven when they knocked off for the day. She packed up her computer, along with all the paperwork that had been generated.

"Tired?" Nick asked as they walked out of the building together.

"Yeah, I am. I'm ready to zap something in the microwave, eat and then drop into bed," she admitted.

"Looks like we could get a downpour," he said. The night was dark and overcast with storm clouds as he walked her to her car. The forecast was for thunderstorms overnight.

"I just hope whatever storms we get don't keep me awake," she replied.

They reached her car and she put her computer and their paperwork in the passenger seat and then straightened back up and turned to him.

There was a simmering tension between them that had only grown with each day that passed. She felt it and she knew he did, too. There were moments when their gazes would lock and she saw his desire for her in the depths of his beautiful gray eyes.

She saw it now, shining with a hunger that burned

in her blood, into her very soul. “Nick…” she whispered softly.

“Ah, Sarah, what are you doing to me?” He gathered her into his arms and kissed her.

She molded her body close against his as she wrapped her arms around his neck. Their tongues danced together in a fiery kiss that drove all other thoughts out of her mind.

The kiss went on for several long, wonderful moments and then he stepped away from her. The hunger was still there in his eyes as he pulled her back against his chest.

“Woman, you drive me crazy,” he finally said as he stroked his fingers through her hair.

“You drive me just as crazy,” she replied softly.

“You know we can’t go there again,” he finally said, and released his hold on her.

She didn’t know that, but she wasn’t going to throw herself at him. He was trying to be as professional as possible and she didn’t want to take that away from him. But this was so miserably hard because she wanted him again so badly.

It was a few minutes later when she was driving home that she realized she was in love with Nick. The knowledge filled her heart with joy and happiness. After Brent she hadn’t thought she would ever love again. She hadn’t believed she would ever be capable of falling in love again.

Nick was not only the man she loved, but he had

also become her best friend. She felt as if she could talk to him about anything and everything and in fact, they had shared both serious conversation and silly ones that had made them both laugh.

However, her happiness at realizing she was in love with Nick was short-lived. She had no idea how he felt about her. Oh, she knew he was into her sexually, but how did he feel about her aside from their terrific sexual chemistry?

She released a tired sigh as she pulled into her garage. She parked and then grabbed her things from the passenger seat and got out. She entered the house and put her computer and the paperwork at one end of her kitchen table and then she headed directly to the freezer to see what was for supper.

She grabbed a fried chicken dinner and got it working in the microwave. While it cooked, she grabbed a soda and popped it open. She took off her holster and gun and then sank down at the table.

God, she was so exhausted. The late nights were definitely starting to catch up to her. Hopefully a good night's sleep tonight would remedy that.

The microwave dinged, announcing that her dinner was ready. She ate in record time and then headed for the shower. It was only when she was under the spray of warm water that she thought about Nick once again.

She had a feeling that they were getting very close to catching the killer and then Nick would be gone. He'd already told her he had no intention of becoming a husband again. What more did she need to know to realize her relationship with him was doomed?

By the time she got into bed she was too exhausted to think about anything anymore. She allowed her soft mattress to envelop her and almost immediately she was asleep.

She jerked awake and bolted to a sitting position, her heart pounding a million beats a minute. A flash of lightning was followed by another boom of thunder that rent the silence of the night. The thunder must have been what had awakened her. She relaxed and drew in several deep breaths to calm the rapid beat of her heart.

As the lightning shot off again, her heart suddenly stopped beating as she let out a small gasp. She could swear that a dark figure just darted past her doorway. Had it only been a figment of her imagination, a trick of the light, or was somebody really in her house?

Her heart resumed a frantic rhythm as she slowly slid out of bed. What should she do? Damn, her gun was in the kitchen on top of the table. Should she call for help? Was there really somebody in her house? Who and why?

For a long moment she stood next to the bed, frozen by fear and yet needing to know if she wasn't alone. She grabbed her cell phone and held it tightly in her hand.

Was it possible she was being robbed? She really didn't have anything worth stealing other than her television. She supposed somebody could pawn that for a little bit of extra money.

She didn't care about her television, what she did care about was that somebody was in her home…in her sanctuary. Was the person dangerous? Oh God, what should she do? The last thing she wanted to do was call for help when she didn't need it.

With a deep breath she stepped into the hallway and turned on the light. Another rumble of thunder sounded, adding to her frantic anxiety. There was nobody in the hallway and she also heard nothing.

Maybe it really had been a figment of her imagination. Maybe there had been no dark figure at all. Maybe it had just been a trick of the lightning. She continued down the hallway, looking carefully in each room she passed and turning on all the lights.

Surely if she were being robbed, the lights would scare the person away. She finally stepped into the living room and gasped as a man in dark clothes and a ski mask rushed toward her from the kitchen.

He shoved her so hard she fell back on the floor, crying out with pain as the back of her head and her body made contact with the carpeting.

Before she could get up, the person flew out her front door and disappeared into the night. She finally got to her feet, her head pounding as she sobbed and closed and locked the door.

Who was the man? Oh God, what had just happened? Who was he and why had he been in her house? She'd scarcely gotten a look at him but with the ski mask on there had been no way for her to identify him.

She still didn't feel safe. With tears falling down her cheeks, she hurried into the kitchen to get her gun.

As she flipped on the kitchen light, she gasped once again. Her gun was still on the table, but her computer and the paperwork were gone.

Chapter Nine

Nick stood next to Sarah and fought the need to pull her into his arms. She looked so small and so vulnerable as she watched Gravois and Officers Judd Lynons and Jason Richards check out the broken window in the bedroom that served as her office.

Apparently, that had been how the thief had gotten into the house. The idea of her being in the house all alone while somebody had come in half terrified Nick for her.

It could have all gone so terribly wrong. It was bad enough that the man had shoved her to the floor. Thank God he hadn't shot her, or fought with her. What would have happened if she'd gotten to her feet and had really confronted him?

"I'm not managing to lift any prints from anywhere on the window," Lynons said in frustration after having tried for several minutes.

"I'm sure he was probably wearing gloves," Nick replied.

"Let's move into the kitchen and see if we can get something pulled off the table," Gravois said.

They all congregated in the kitchen and Lynons got to work fingerprinting the table. Once again Nick wanted to draw Sarah into his arms. What chilled him to the bone was he had a feeling that tonight she had shared her house with the Honey Island Swamp Monster murderer.

The killer had obviously decided that their investigation was hitting too close to home and so he'd stolen the very work notes and the computer that might have pointed to him.

It was the only thing that made sense. And whoever the killer was, he must have a deep enough bond with Sarah that he hadn't wanted to really harm her.

There was no question that the loss of the paperwork and the computer would set the investigation back a bit, but at the moment he was more worried about Sarah's well-being.

She was clad in her pink nightgown and a short white robe. Her face was unusually pale and her entire body appeared to tremble. When she'd called him and told him her house had been broken into, he couldn't get to her fast enough. He'd heard the fear in her voice and all he'd wanted to do was get to her as quickly as possible.

Lynons managed to lift a bunch of fingerprints off the table but they all appeared the same and everyone was sure they probably belonged to Sarah.

Her fingerprints were on file with the department so it would be easy to check for certain.

The storm overhead had passed and it was after two thirty when everyone finally left. The moment they all stepped out the front door, Nick closed and locked it and then went to Sarah, who stood still as a statue by the coffee table.

He immediately pulled her into his arms, holding her tight as she trembled against his chest. She began to cry softly. "It's okay," he whispered to her. "You're okay now."

She continued to cry for several more minutes and then with a deep sigh she stepped back from him. She sank down on the sofa and he sat next to her.

"When I realized somebody was in the house with me, I got so scared," she said, her voice trembling a bit. "And then when I saw him and he pushed me, I was in shock. Then I saw the computer and everything was gone and I realized the man who had come into my house was probably the killer."

"Thank God you weren't seriously hurt," he said as he took one of her hands in his. "Thank God, you didn't jump up and run after him." The idea of her being killed shot an iciness through him.

"Now that it's all over I'm also so damned mad." She gazed at him with sad eyes. "He got all of our work product…everything."

"We can generate all that again," he replied.

"Who is this person? And why steal all our things now?"

"The killer was desperate to see exactly what we were doing," he replied. "I think our killer must have seen that you downloaded all the schedules and that scared him. It let him know that all the cops in the department were suspects."

He squeezed her hand. "He wanted our work notes to see if we had narrowed down anything. If it's any consolation at all, he must have a friendship with you and that's what kept you alive tonight."

"That is no consolation at all," she replied, some of the fire back in her eyes. "I want this bastard behind bars and I don't give a damn if I have a friendship with him or not. He's sick and perverted. The way he kills these women make him a monstrosity."

"I've been trying to work up a psychological profile of the killer and why he would want to basically erase his victim's faces," he said.

"He obviously hates women," she replied.

"True, but the psychology goes much deeper than that. Maybe he's trying to replace somebody and when he gets them to his kill place, he's angry that they don't look like what he wants...what he needs."

"Mommy issues?" she suggested.

"Maybe," he replied. "Now, do you have something I can use to board up that broken window in your office?" He released his hold on her hand and stood.

"There are some old pieces of plywood in the garage. They were there when I bought the house." She also got up from the sofa. "I'll get you a hammer and some nails."

Thirty minutes later the window was boarded up, but he was still reluctant to leave her and he could tell she didn't want him to go.

"Do you want me to stay for the rest of the night with you?" he asked.

"Would you mind?" Her gaze was soft and faintly needy. She'd been through a frightening ordeal and he could understand her not wanting to be alone right now.

"Of course I wouldn't mind," he replied, and smiled at her. "When my partner needs me, I'm there."

"Thank you, Nick."

Fifteen minutes later they were in bed and she snuggled into his arms. As always, the desire she stoked in him rose to the surface but he fought against it. Thankfully, it didn't take her long to fall asleep and he soon followed.

He awoke at some point later. The room was still dark, and even though he was still half-asleep, Sarah's body moved against his and he was fully aroused.

Clothes disappeared and warm limbs wound around each other. Her small gasps of pleasure whispered in the room. It was as if he were in a dream as they slowly made love. It was a wonderful dream. He felt as if he belonged here with her and then he was sleeping once again.

When he awakened again it was a few minutes after seven. He was spooned around Sarah and they both were naked, letting him know that what he'd thought was a wonderful dream had really been a reality. They had made love once again.

Damn, his body was a traitorous thing. Apparently even in sleep he wanted her and she wanted him. He slowly moved back from her warm sweetness and slid out of the bed. She stirred, but didn't awaken, which he was grateful for. She needed to sleep.

He stood next to the bed for several moments and simply gazed at her in the golden morning light that flowed in through the window.

The illumination shone in her tousled hair, turning it into a soft halo around her head. Her lips were slightly parted, as if just awaiting his kiss. She was so beautiful even in slumber.

He loved her wide-eyed wonder when he taught her something new and he adored her when she laughed over something funny. He loved talking to her about anything and nothing.

With a frown he grabbed his jeans and T-shirt off the floor and left the room. He dressed quickly in the bathroom and then quietly left the house.

As he drove to Nene's place, he realized with a jolt that he was in love with his partner. He didn't know when he'd fallen for her. He didn't know if it had been when she'd landed in the swamp while enthusiastically chasing James Noman, or if it had been when she'd held his hand after he'd shared his childhood trauma with her.

He didn't know when it had happened, but it had. He was crazy in love with Sarah. The thought brought him no happiness. There was still no future for the two of them. He had no intention of seeking a relationship with her once these murders were solved.

What he'd done last night by making love with her once again was give her hope. He had a feeling she was totally into him. The signs had been there with her…the way she looked at him and how she touched him when it wasn't necessary. Yeah, he knew she had deep feelings for him.

However, the worst thing he could do was plan a life with her. He knew what he was and he would never want Sarah to suffer his flaws. She definitely deserved so much better than him.

When he reached Nene's, the older woman met him at the door. "Is Sarah okay?" she immediately asked, her eyes filled with a wealth of concern.

"She's fine," he replied. "News definitely flies fast in this town."

"The gossips were busy this morning. A break-in must be a frightening thing," Nene said. "Poor Sarah, I'm sure she was scared to death."

"She was definitely frightened, but thank God she was unharmed physically," he replied.

"Thank God for that. Snakes in your bedroom and then a break-in…you've really shaken somebody up." She shook her head.

"I guess we have," he agreed.

She looked at him slyly. "At least Sarah has you by her side, just like in a good romance novel."

"Unfortunately, this isn't a romance novel," he replied.

She released a deep sigh. "Well, I won't keep you any longer. I know how busy you must be but I just wanted to make sure Sarah was okay. She's a lovely woman and has always been very kind to me."

He smiled at her. "Yeah, I'm just on my way upstairs for a quick shower and then I need to head back into the office again."

"I certainly hope you catch this man," she said.

"We will, Nene," he replied firmly.

"There are some blueberry muffins in the kitchen if you want to grab one to take with you," she said. "In fact, take two and give one to Sarah."

"Thanks, I just might want to do that." He headed for the staircase and she went into the kitchen. It took him only minutes to shower and then dress in a clean pair of navy slacks and a navy polo.

On his way out he detoured into the kitchen where Nene wrapped up two of the huge muffins for him to take and then he was on his way back to the office.

He had no idea when to expect Sarah. He hoped she slept as long as she needed, long enough to feel refreshed and ready to go again. They'd both been working long hours with plenty of nighttime interruptions. He was used to this kind of a schedule when working a case, but he knew she wasn't.

Once he reached the station he went into their little office, grabbed a fresh notepad from the filing cabinet and then sank down at the table.

Whoever the thief was that had stolen the computer and paperwork must have believed that it would stymie the investigation for weeks to come. But they hadn't stolen Nick's mind and his memory.

The notes that had been on the computer were still fairly fresh in his mind. He began to make a list of the men on the force that they hadn't been able to alibi with work for the nights of the murders. As he worked, he ate one of the muffins, which was delicious.

He'd written down several names when the door opened and Sarah came in.

"Sorry I'm late, partner," she said, and took the seat opposite him with her usual beautiful smile.

"You aren't late," he replied. "How are you feeling?"

"Rested and ready to get back to work."

He was relieved that apparently they weren't going to talk about their lovemaking in the middle of the night. What was there to say about it? It had happened and it had been wonderful, but it had also been another mistake. He had a feeling she wouldn't want to hear that.

"I've just been sitting here writing down all the names of the officers who we couldn't find an alibi for on the nights of the murders," he explained. "Thankfully a lot of our work is still fresh in my mind."

"Let me see who you have so far." She moved into the chair next to his and pulled it closer to him. With his love for her burning hot in his chest, everything about her nearness right now was sheer torture.

The soft curve of her cheek…the plump lusciousness of her lips and the scent that belonged to her alone…he had a feeling they would all…that she would haunt him for a very long time to come after he left this little town.

She added a few more names to the list he'd made and then pushed the remaining muffin before her. "A gift for you from Nene," he said.

"That was nice of her, but where's yours?"

"Gee, I don't know what happened to it," he said.

She grinned at him. "That story would be much easier to believe if you didn't wear the evidence in the form of muffin crumbles on your chin."

"Busted." He laughed and quickly brushed off his chin.

Their levity didn't last long as he leaned back in his chair. "You know we can't keep this investigation a secret any longer," he said as she ate her muffin.

"I know," she replied solemnly.

"It's time for us to start interrogating some of these officers."

"I'm not looking forward to it. I still can't believe one of the officers I've worked with here is a suspect," she replied, and shoved the last of the muffin away.

He looked at her equally solemnly. "I truly believe in my gut that a cop is not only our suspect, but one of them is definitely the Honey Island Swamp Monster murderer," he replied.

"I THINK BEFORE we go any further, we need to let Gravois know where our investigation has led us," Nick said.

"Should we go to speak to him now?" Sarah asked. She was torn between the dread of finding out who among them was the monster and wanting to get the monster behind bars as soon as possible.

That wasn't the only thing she was torn about since awakening that morning. She and Nick had made love again last night. It had been slow and sleepy and beyond wonderful.

He had to love her just a little bit. He didn't strike her as the kind of guy who would have sex with absolutely no feelings behind it. In one of their many talks he had told her he had been completely faithful in his marriage and she believed that of him.

He was the man she wanted for the rest of her

life. She was drawn to so many qualities about him and she could easily imagine marrying him and living happily ever after. They would share their love of crime stories and she would give him babies. It would be perfect…except it wasn't.

"Yeah, let's head down to Gravois's office now," he replied.

As she followed him down the hallway, she knew there would come a time when she would tell him exactly how she felt about him. She couldn't let him leave Black Bayou without him knowing the depths of her love for him. But before that could happen, they had a killer to catch…a killer that at this very moment might be in the building with them.

Nick rapped on Gravois's door and after Gravois called enter, they both did. "We need to speak with you," Nick said somberly.

"Then come in." Gravois gestured them into the chairs in front of his desk. "What's going on? Is there a break in the case?"

"We're getting very close. We believe that the killer is a cop here in the department," Nick said.

Gravois reeled back in his chair with obvious stunned surprise. His features paled and then filled with a ruddy color. He leaned forward and frowned. "Are you absolutely sure about that?"

"As sure as we can be," Sarah replied grimly.

"A cop would easily be able to get those women to come with him out of the swamp. He would also know the best areas in town to dump the bodies, and he'd know about forensics," Nick said.

"And then we have that piece of material which is the same makeup as the officers' shirts," Sarah added.

"All of our other suspects had been cleared, leaving us to believe one of your officers is our killer," Nick said.

"I'll be a son of a bitch," Gravois said. "Do you have a specific suspect in mind?"

"No, not yet," Nick replied.

"So, what do you need from me?" Gravois asked.

"We have a list of officers we'd like to start interrogating," Nick explained. "I'm trained in interrogation and hopefully I'll get a tell from the guilty party along with some evidence."

"We certainly don't expect anyone to confess, but we need to find out who has solid alibis for the nights of the murders and who doesn't," Sarah said.

"I'll make sure all the officers know they are to fully cooperate with you," Gravois replied.

"We appreciate that, but we'd like to start the interviews immediately with the men who are on duty today," Nick replied.

Gravois nodded. "That's fine with me, but please keep me in the loop. If you get a solid suspect, then dammit, I want to know."

"By all means, we'll definitely keep you in the loop," Nick said as he rose to his feet. Sarah stood as well and minutes later she and Nick were back in their little room.

The first officer they pulled in for an interrogation was Judd Lynons. He hadn't been working on the nights of the murders but he was working today.

Sarah went into the officers' room where Judd sat at a desk eating a candy bar from the vending machine. "Hey, Judd."

"Hey, Sarah." He smiled at her. Judd was in his mid-thirties and was physically fit with broad shoulders and big arms. He was big and strong enough to carry a victim.

"Could you come with me into our office for a few minutes?"

His smile faded into a look of curiosity. "Uh… sure." He took the last bite of his candy bar, crinkled up the wrapper and threw it away and then got up from the desk and followed her down the hallway.

Nick stood as they entered the room and then he gestured Judd into a chair at the table. "What's going on here?" Judd asked in confusion. "Why do you need to talk to me?"

"We're in the process of narrowing down our pool of suspects," Nick said.

Judd looked at Sarah and then at Nick in astonishment. "Am I a suspect?"

"We're going to be talking to all the officers over the next couple of days," Nick said.

Judd's eyes widened. "You think a cop did those

murders? Man, that's messed up." He shook his head and settled back in the chair. "If you have questions for me, then ask away. I don't have anything to hide."

"We understand that you grew up for the first ten years of your life in the swamp," Nick said.

And so, the first interrogation began. Judd appeared to be open and honest and provided an alibi for the night of the fourth murder that they could easily check out. According to him, he'd been in Shreveport for a buddy's wedding and he had the hotel records to prove that fact.

If his alibi checked out, then he wasn't their killer. They knew without a doubt that the same man had killed all the women, so if somebody had a solid alibi for one of the murders that exonerated them from being the person they sought.

"If you get a chance later today or tomorrow, please bring us the receipts you have," Nick said to Judd.

"And the names and phone numbers of some of the people who were with you in Shreveport," Sarah added.

"I definitely will," Judd replied. "Does that mean you're finished with me?"

"For now," Nick replied.

A moment later Judd was gone. Sarah frowned as she saw who they next needed to talk to. "Ryan and I grew up together. I can't imagine him doing something like this. He might be a total jerk, but I can't imagine him being our killer."

Nick reached across the table and covered her hand with his. "You knew this was going to be difficult. I'm so sorry, Sarah, that one of these men you've viewed as your friend and coworker is probably a serial killer." He squeezed her hand and then released it. "But at this point in the investigation, it's important to keep an open mind."

She definitely appreciated the gesture and his support. "So, now I'll go get Ryan." She got out of her chair, left their little space and then went back to the officers' workroom.

Apparently, Judd hadn't returned to the workroom. He might be in the break room or he might have been called out for something. Whatever the case, Ryan was alone reading something on his phone when she went in to get him.

"Hey, Ryan, you want to come with me to speak with Nick?"

"Speak to him about what?" he asked.

"You'll find out when you get there," she replied.

He shrugged his shoulders and turned off his phone. He then rose from the table and grinned at her. "You know I'll follow you anywhere, Short-Stuff."

Sarah sighed, but was grateful he followed her back down the hallway silently. Ryan had worked several of the murders, but they needed to know what he'd done in the hours before the bodies had been found. It would have been easy for him to kill a woman and then show up a couple of hours later on duty. There were two murders that he hadn't been on duty for and hadn't been called in for.

"Hey, man," Ryan said in greeting to Nick.

"Officer Staub...please have a seat. We have some questions to ask you," Nick said.

"And I'm sure I have some answers for you," Ryan said flippantly.

"Where were you in the hours before you showed up to work the Soulange murder?" Nick asked.

Ryan looked first at Nick and then at Sarah in surprise. He then leaned back in his chair and laughed. "Is this some kind of a joke?" he finally asked.

"It's absolutely no joke," Sarah replied.

"You really think I'm the big, bad killer you're looking for?" He turned his gaze once again on Sarah. "Short-Stuff, you should know better than this."

"Her name is Sarah or Officer Beauregard." Nick's eyes were the color of dark storms. "If I hear you diminish her name or stature again within this department, I'll file a lawsuit on her behalf."

Ryan stopped laughing and met Nick's gaze. "Oh, give it a rest, tough guy. You aren't going to do that."

"Try me. You'll find out that I don't play," Nick said with a deadly calm.

"Sarah doesn't mind if I tease her," Ryan said with a little less assurance in his voice.

"Actually, Ryan, I do mind," she said.

"Duly noted," he replied to her. "I'm sorry if I've hurt you." His mouth said the words, but his blue eyes were a dark shade that she'd never seen there before. He didn't look sorry. He looked angry.

Was it really possible the man who had been asking her out for the past couple of months was the Honey Island Swamp Monster murderer?

Chapter Ten

Ryan was unable to provide a solid alibi for any of the nights of the murders. He thought he was on a date before one of the murders and then he said he was home alone and in bed. He needed to check his planner to see where he might have been and who he might have been with. He'd have to get back with them.

When he left their room, Sarah released a deep sigh. "God, he sounded guilty as hell," she said.

"Maybe…maybe not," Nick said. "A lot of innocent people when put on the spot can't name what they were doing on any particular night."

"But on several of those nights he investigated heinous murders, you would think his activities for those nights would be burned in his brain," she protested.

"We'll see what kind of alibis he can provide once he checks his planner," Nick replied.

"Planner, my butt," she retorted.

Nick laughed. "You don't believe he has a daily planner?"

"He has a daily planner like I have a flying blue dog," she replied, making Nick laugh again.

"We'll see if he can provide us something tomorrow," he said.

Sarah appeared utterly miserable and again Nick recognized how difficult this all must be for her. These were men she'd worked with, fellow officers she'd considered friends.

"I keep going over and over it again in my mind," she said with obvious frustration. "If one of the officers really is our killer then why didn't I get a sense of that kind of darkness in him? Why didn't I feel something off about him?"

"Sarah, honey, hiding in plain sight, that's what these kind of people…that's what these kinds of killers are good at. He's a cool customer and he definitely believes he's much smarter than us."

"Is he? I mean, is it possible we won't ever be able to identify him?" Her eyes simmered with a wealth of worry.

Nick took her hand in his. "We're going to get him, Sarah. He doesn't realize he's up against a partnership better than Batman and Robin, smarter than Sherlock and Dr. Watson and more tenacious than Scooby-Doo and Shaggy."

She immediately laughed at his silliness, which was exactly what he wanted. He loved the sound of her laughter and the fact that the darkness that had been in her eyes was momentarily gone. He squeezed her hand and then released it. "You can't give up now, Sarah. We're so close and when we do get him, think of all the young lives we'll be saving."

She sighed once again. "I only wish you would have been brought in earlier," she replied. "Then maybe he would have been taken off the streets much sooner and some of these women would still be alive."

"Unfortunately, we can't go back in time, but we're here now and we're getting closer and closer. Now, who should we talk to next?"

He still saw how troubled she was, but he couldn't do anything to make this process easier on her. He wished he could, but the truth was he couldn't. Still, the torment in her eyes hurt him for her.

They did one more interview and then stopped for a quick lunch of burgers from a drive-through called Big Larry's. After eating they interviewed two more officers.

There were no other officers in house to speak with and so for the rest of the afternoon they made phone calls and scheduled interviews for the next day with some of the men who worked nights.

It was just after six when he sent Sarah home. They would have a full day the next day as they tried to get to as many officers as possible.

Once Sarah was gone, the scent of her lingered

in the room. She had to know he was more than a little crazy about her. Surely she'd seen his emotions for her shining from his eyes when he gazed at her. Surely she felt it whenever he touched her even in the simplest way.

However, sometimes love just wasn't enough. He had loved Amy when he'd married her, but his love hadn't been enough to keep his marriage intact. When it came to relationships, he was a total loser and Sarah deserved far more than a loser in her life.

His mind shifted to the interviews they had conducted so far that day. He'd been trained in interrogation techniques and how to read body language. So far today none of the men had given him the tells that they were lying in any way.

Ryan had come closest as he'd deflected a lot during the questioning and his body language had been closed off and defensive. Nick was eager to see what kind of receipts Ryan brought the next day as alibis for any of the nights of the murders.

Unbeknownst to Sarah, Nick had another suspect in mind, one that she'd already firmly rejected as a possibility. Gravois. The name now thundered in his brain.

Was it possible Gravois hadn't worked too hard in solving these murders because he didn't want them solved? As much as Nick had seen a lot of growth in Sarah, why would Gravois partner him with the least experienced officer in the department? Somebody who hadn't worked on any of the previous murder investigations?

Gravois was physically strong enough to carry the women out of the swamp and to a kill place. He would then be strong enough to take them to the places where their bodies had been found. The women would willingly interact with the head lawman without protest.

Still, Nick didn't intend to jump to any conclusions where Gravois was concerned. He would continue to exclude all the other men in the department and only then would he come at Gravois.

He didn't know how long he sat there lost in his thoughts, but he finally got up from the table and headed for the building's back door.

It was another gray evening with dark clouds hiding the sunlight and gloomy shadows taking over the landscape. He had just reached the driver side of his car when a gunshot fired off. He automatically hit the ground, aware that the bullet slammed into the driver door of his car.

He grabbed his gun as adrenaline fired through his entire body. Two cars over he saw some movement. He didn't return fire…at least not yet. Right now, he realized he was a sitting duck where he was and he needed to move around his car for more cover.

He started to rise to a crouch, but another bullet flew mere inches by his head to hit his car door once again. He dropped down and slithered like a snake on the ground to get around his car bumper and only then did he return fire by shooting twice in the direction where he'd seen the movement.

What the hell? Who was shooting at him? He waited, his heart beating frantically. He shot a quick glance around the bumper but saw no more movement.

The shadows were deepening by the minute. Was the shooter still there? Just waiting for him to leave his cover? Had the person moved to a different location where he could get off another shot?

He looked to his left and then his right, unsure where danger might come from next. He tightened his grip on his gun, ready to fire again if necessary.

Seconds turned into long minutes and nothing more happened. There were no more gunshots but still, Nick was reluctant to move from his cover.

At that moment the back door of the building flew open and Officer Colby Shanks stepped out. He was nothing but a kid and the last thing Nick wanted was for him to somehow get hurt.

"Get back inside, Shanks. There's an active shooter in the parking lot," Nick yelled.

Instead of going back inside, the kid dropped into a crouching position and pulled his gun. "Where is he?" He pointed his weapon first to the left and then to the right.

By that time Nick had a feeling the danger had passed. Slowly he rose to his feet. Somebody had just tried to kill him. There was no doubt in his mind that the Honey Island Swamp Monster murderer was or had been in this parking lot with him and wanted him dead. That was a sure way to stop the investigation.

SARAH HAD USED her evening to try to de-stress. She'd taken a long, hot lilac-scented bath and then had baked a seasoned chicken breast and had added steamed broccoli for dinner.

She'd then sunk down on the sofa and had turned her television to a comedy show she occasionally watched. The show had just begun when Nick called.

Oh God, please not another body, she thought as she hit Pause on the remote and then answered. "Hey, partner, what's up?"

Nick never called her unless something had happened.

"Not much, I just decided to give you a call and make sure you were doing okay," he replied.

She frowned. Something had happened. She felt it in her bones. The phone call was completely out of character for him. "Okay, Nick…what's really going on? You've never called me before just to check on my well-being."

There was a long pause and then she heard him sigh. "I played a part in the gunfight at OK Corral tonight, only it happened in the station parking lot as I got to my car."

"What?" She tightened her fingers around her phone. "Are you okay?"

"Yeah, I'm fine. Thankfully whoever it was wasn't a terrific shot. He fired on me twice and missed and by that time I'd managed to move to some cover. Then Shanks came out of the back door and the shooter disappeared."

"Do you have any idea who it was?" she asked.

"Yeah, it was our killer. Am I certain who he is? No. I didn't get a look at him."

"Did you go in and report it to Gravois?"

"I attempted to, but he'd already left for the day. Ryan was also gone."

Even though his voice held no judgment, the pit of her stomach burned with anxiety. There was still no way she believed Gravois had anything to do with the murders, but she couldn't say that for sure about Ryan.

"Anyway," he continued, "I just wanted to call and make sure you were okay."

"Let's be honest, Nick. The killer wants the investigation to stop and he obviously doesn't see me as any kind of a threat. I'm just Officer Beauregard, who passes out speeding tickets and sits on the desk."

"The biggest mistake the killer can make is to

underestimate you," he replied. "But you need to make me a promise, Sarah."

"What?"

"You need to promise me that if anything happens to me, you'll go on fighting to find this killer," he said.

"Nothing is going to happen to you, Nick," she protested. She didn't even want to think about him being hurt or killed. Her heart wouldn't be able to stand it.

"Just promise me, Sarah," he replied pleadingly.

"Okay, okay… I promise," she replied. "Maybe I should be your bodyguard as well as your partner," she said more than half-seriously. "I could pick you up in the mornings and drive you home in the evenings. With the two of us together, it would be far more difficult for somebody to attack you. Please, Nick…let's do that."

"I don't want to place you in any risk," he protested.

"We'll protect each other. So, it's settled, I'll pick you up in the morning at around seven."

His low laughter filled the line. "You are one stubborn woman."

"Yes, I am, when something matters to me, and you matter," she replied. "So I'll see you in the morning at Nene's and in the meantime, stay safe, Nick," she said, fighting against the words she really wanted to say.

She wanted to tell him that she loved him with all her heart and soul and that she couldn't imagine her life without him. But she also knew in her heart and soul that now wasn't the time for him to hear those words from her. He'd just been attacked by the killer, involved in a gunfight. The mood definitely wasn't right now for a romantic confession.

"Okay, partner, I'll see you in the morning," he replied, and with that they hung up.

The relaxation she'd found earlier in the evening was now gone, destroyed by the fact that somebody had tried to kill Nick in the parking lot.

Had it been Ryan? Or had it been another officer, one they had yet to interview? She didn't have the answer. All she knew was somebody had lain in wait for Nick and tried to kill him.

Chills raced down her spine. The stakes had been high to begin with in this case, but with the killer trying to take out Nick, the stakes had now shot through the ceiling.

The next morning, she pulled into Nene's driveway at ten after seven. Nick immediately walked out the front door, letting her know he'd been watching for her.

He got into the passenger side and grinned at her. "I have to say, you're one of the prettiest bodyguards I've ever seen."

She laughed. "Don't let all this prettiness fool you. I'm a mean bitch when it comes to protecting those I love." Realizing what she'd just said, she quickly pulled out of the driveway.

"We're going to have a long day," he said as she turned onto Main Street. "We've got a lot of interviews lined up for today but the good news is we'll only have four left to do tomorrow."

"And then we check out all the alibis and see where we're at," she replied.

"Exactly," he agreed. "I'd say within the next week we'll be able to name our killer."

"I hope so, and I hope there isn't another murder in the meantime," she replied.

If the case ended in a week, then it would be time for him to leave. What she wanted to tell him was how badly she'd miss him. She'd miss their deep conversations and their shared laughter. She would miss his touch and his warm smiles. God, she would miss everything about him.

However, she said none of that. But she was determined that before he left Black Bayou, he would know how much she loved him, how deeply she was in love with him.

They made one stop on the way in at a small bakery where they got tall cups of coffee for themselves and two dozen doughnuts. "We'll offer the officers a doughnut and while they enjoy the sweet, we'll dig deep into their heads," Nick said.

By the time they got to the office, the first officer on their list of interviews had arrived. Bart

Kurby worked nights and Sarah didn't know him very well. On the nights of the murders, he'd been off work.

He was a tall, middle-aged man, physically fit and with dark, hooded eyes. He sat at their table and didn't accept their offer of a doughnut.

He appeared tired and impatient as it was past time for him to go home and get some sleep after being on duty all night long. "We'd like to talk to you about the nights of the murders," Nick said.

"Yeah, I heard you were talking to everyone in the department," Bart replied. "I can't believe you two really think one of us is the Honey Island Swamp Monster."

"We're just following where the evidence takes us," Sarah said.

He shot her a quick glance and then looked back at Nick. "So, what do you want to know from me?"

Sarah frowned. The man had dismissed her with that single look and it definitely irritated her. Apparently, Nick had caught it, too, for he looked at her and gave an imperceptible nod of his head.

"Bart, we have seen from scheduling that you weren't working on the nights of the murders. We need to know what you were doing on those nights between the hours of about six and one in the morning," Sarah said with as much authority as she could muster.

Bart looked at her once again, this time with a

little more interest. "I think on most of the nights, I would have been in bed by about nine in the evening."

"Anybody in bed with you?" she asked. She did know that Bart wasn't married.

He raised a dark eyebrow. "I'm really not the type to kiss and tell."

"Better to kiss and tell than wind up in prison for murders you didn't commit," she replied.

He hesitated a long moment. "Fine, on the night of the last murder I was with Paula Kincaid. We were together all evening and she spent the night at my place."

"Speaking of places, we know you live in an apartment here in town, but you also own a property just outside of town. What is that?" she asked.

"That's my parents' old place. I've been working on it and plan to move in there within the next couple of months," he said.

"Okay, I think that's all we need from you right now," she said, and stood to dismiss the man.

"Good work, partner," Nick said as soon as Bart left.

"He definitely ticked me off by dismissing me. Thanks for letting me do the interview," she replied.

"No problem, you did a good job."

"Thanks. You know what's really interesting? Paula Kincaid is supposedly happily married to George Kincaid, who travels for business. I wonder if push comes to shove, she'll substantiate Bart's alibi."

"Time will tell, and speaking of time, our next officer should be ready to be interviewed," Nick replied.

And so, the day passed. It was half past six by the time they were finished. There were two doughnuts left in the box and Sarah's head was filled with all the information they'd garnered that day.

"How about dinner at the café," Nick suggested as they packed up their notes to leave.

"Sounds good to me," she agreed. Together they left the station and got into her car.

"While we eat, we can talk about everything we learned today," he said once they were headed to the café.

"Good, because my brain feels like it's about to explode with all the new information," she replied. "I'm hoping you can help me make sense of it all."

"I'll do my best, but I was hoping you could help me make sense of it all," he replied with a small laugh.

Fifteen minutes later they were seated at the café and had ordered their dinner. He reached across the table and took her hand in his. She loved when he held her hand, and he did it often.

"I'm so proud of you, Sarah," he said. His beautiful gray eyes held her gaze intently as his thumb rubbed back and forth on her hand. "You've come a long way since you took that bath in the swamp."

She laughed. "There was really no other way than up at that point." Warm shivers stole up her spine as he continued to make love to her hand with his.

"Seriously, you've become a formidable officer and I hope that when all this is over, you aren't handing out tickets or stuck on the dispatch desk. You deserve to be working on criminal cases."

He released her hand only when their food arrived. They had both ordered burgers and fries and for the next hour and a half they ate and talked about the suspects they had interviewed that day.

"What I find so interesting about today is that Ryan didn't bring us any alibis," he said.

Sarah dragged a fry through the pool of ketchup on her plate. "Maybe he lost his day planner," she replied drily.

Nick laughed but sobered quickly. "If he doesn't bring us anything tomorrow, then we need to pull him in for a less friendly interview."

"Sounds like a plan," she agreed. "I want this killer caught and if it's Ryan, then he deserves to go to prison."

"Whoever it is, he's going to be spending the rest of his life in prison. You look tired," he said as they finished up the meal.

"I am," she admitted. "I just need a good night's sleep and then I'll be ready to go hard in the morning."

Minutes later they left the café and as they walked to her car, his hand once again sought hers. He had to love her, she thought. He had to love her more than a little bit. He reached to touch her far too often for this relationship to be strictly partners in crime solving.

None of that mattered as they reached her car and he got into the passenger side while she got behind the wheel. "What about you? Are you tired?" she asked.

"Yeah, I am, but like you all I need is a good night's sleep and I'll be ready to go again."

They were quiet on the ride to Nene's and within minutes he was gone, leaving only the scent of his cologne behind. She had no idea where they would go after the investigation was over and the killer was behind bars.

He'd already told her he never wanted to be a husband again and Sarah was at a place in her life where she didn't want to settle for less. She wanted a husband and children. She wanted a family. Ever since her parents had died, she'd had a desire to build her own family.

She couldn't think about all this right now. They had a killer to catch and then she'd see what happened with Nick. Still, no matter how she twisted things in her head where he was concerned, she just didn't see a happy ending.

Chapter Eleven

Sarah's head now was filled with alibis and questions concerning all the men they'd spoken to that day. Even talking to Nick over dinner hadn't managed to quiet the chaos in her head.

She got home and pulled into her garage, then entered her house. She dropped her car keys on the table but carried her gun back to the bedroom. She didn't intend to make the mistake of being without her gun at night ever again.

After a quick shower, she got into her nightgown and crawled into bed. As always, her mattress embraced her and within minutes, she was sound asleep.

Her phone woke her. She fumbled for it on the nightstand and noted that it was one o'clock. The call could only be bad news.

She was surprised that the caller identification showed that it was Gravois calling her. She answered. "Gravois?"

"Sarah, I just got a hot tip that the killer is going to act tonight, probably within the next hour or so."

"A hot tip?" She frowned. "A hot tip from who?"

"I'll explain everything when you get here," he said.

"Get where?" She sat up and gripped her phone tighter.

"To the swamp," he said with an urgency in his voice. "You know where the old fallen tree trunk is?"

"Yes, I do."

"Meet me there as quickly as possible. I've already called Nick so there's no reason for you to speak to him. Don't waste any time, Sarah. We're going to get the bastard tonight."

"I'll be there as quickly as possible," she replied.

The minute the call ended she flew into action. As she dressed, she wondered what kind of a tip Gravois had gotten and who was the tipster?

Would they really be able to catch the killer tonight? Oh God, she hoped so. It was past time to get him behind bars, especially before another woman died. She was ready to go within ten minutes and then she got into her car and headed to Vincent's.

The night was unusually dark with a heavy layer of clouds hiding the moon and stars. The streets were deserted so she was able to push the speed limit and arrive at Vincent's in record time.

She didn't see Gravois's or Nick's car in the lot,

but she knew where to go and hopefully the two men would show up quickly.

She decided to shoot a quick text to Nick. Gravois called me and I'm here just waiting for you and him to show up. Tonight, we get him! She sent the text and then got out of her car.

She hesitated before entering the darkness of the swamp. On the one hand she wanted…no, needed to turn on the flashlight on her phone, but on the other hand she didn't want a killer to see her or know she was out here.

With it being so dark, she finally decided to turn on the flashlight and point it directly toward the ground. She didn't want to trip and hurt herself. She wanted to be an active participant in taking down the killer. She'd worked so hard for this.

A tipster. Obviously, somebody knew something about the killer and had decided to contact Gravois with this important information. Hopefully no other woman would die after tonight.

She kept the light shining on the ground and hoped nobody would see her. It didn't take her long to find the fallen tree trunk. Once there, she sat on the trunk and shut off her light.

She tried to listen for the sounds of the two men approaching but the swamp was filled with noises of its own. Bugs buzzed around her head and someplace in the distance, a fish slapped the water. Wind blew through the tops of the trees and little creatures rustled in the brush nearby.

She nearly screamed out when a hand clamped down on her shoulder. She whirled around to see Gravois. "Jeez, you scared me half to death," she whispered.

"Sorry," he replied. His flashlight was on and he shone it on himself.

"What's going on? Are you going to tell me who your tipster is?" she asked, her voice still in a whisper.

"Not right now. According to what he told me, we don't have much time," he replied, also whispering.

"I wonder where Nick is?" she asked.

"I don't know, but we can't wait for him. We need to get in position."

"Is the killer coming in this way?" she asked, a faint chill trying to walk up her spine.

"That's what I was told," he replied. "We need to crouch behind this trunk and hide and wait to see who shows up. I definitely think it's going to be one of the officers."

"Your tipster didn't tell you specifically who it was?" she asked.

"No. I was lucky to get as much information as I did out of him," Gravois replied. "Now, we need to get into position."

Who would it be? Who was going to come into the swamp with another heinous murder on his mind?

She stood to move behind the trunk, but before she could take a step, Gravois slapped her phone out of her hand and then crushed it with his heel.

She stared at him in stunned surprise. "Gravois… wha-what are you doing?"

As she stared at his face, she suddenly realized his eyes were narrowed and his features were tensed in a mask of evil she'd never seen there before. A daze of shock held her in place as her mind grappled to make sense of what was happening.

Danger. Danger. It flashed in her head that she was in trouble. Gravois…it had been him all along. Oh God, he was the Honey Island Swamp Monster murderer.

"Sarah…" he said softly, and then reached out for her. It was then she saw it…a hypodermic needle in his hand. The daze of shock and surprise snapped and she ran. Blindly she raced into the swamp with Gravois on her heels.

She ran for her life. Frantically she sped into the darkness, knowing that if he caught her, she would be the next victim of the monster.

NICK'S NOTIFICATION DING awoke him, indicating he had a text. Who on earth would be texting him at this time of the night?

He grabbed his phone and read the message from Sarah. Gravois called me and I'm here just waiting for you and him to show up. Tonight, we get him!

He read the message twice and then, with his heart pounding, he jumped out of bed and got dressed. Gravois. The name thundered over and over again in Nick's head.

He immediately tried to call her, but it rang and rang and then went to voice mail. He quickly dressed and then strapped on his holster and gun. If Gravois had hurt a hair on Sarah's head Nick would kill the man. Sarah had said she was there and waiting for him, but she hadn't told him where she was.

All he knew for sure was that he believed Sarah was in trouble. Her message had implied that Gravois had contacted him, but that hadn't happened. Yes, Sarah was definitely in danger. If what he believed was right then she was alone with the man who might be the killer.

The swamp. That was the only place that made some sort of insane sense. She had to be there. He jumped into his car and headed out. He continued to try to call her, but all his calls continued to go to her voice mail.

Thank God at a few minutes after one in the morning the streets were deserted, allowing him to get to Vincent's in just a few minutes. And thank God he'd guessed right in coming here as Sarah's car was in the parking lot.

He got out of his car and as he gazed into the dark entrance of the marsh the back of his throat closed up and the familiar high anxiety tightened his chest.

Dammit, he wasn't a frightened little boy anymore. He was a grown man and he needed to go into the swamp and find the woman he loved…a woman he feared was in terrible danger.

With that thought in mind, he swallowed against his fear, turned on the flashlight feature on his phone and headed in. The anxiety he now felt wasn't due to him being in the swamp; rather it was because he needed to find Sarah.

It didn't take him long to reach the old fallen tree trunk and as his flashlight swept the area, it landed on a phone… Sarah's phone. The blood seemed to rush out of his body, leaving him light-headed.

If he needed a physical reason to believe Sarah was in danger this was it. He reached down and picked up the broken phone. He pressed the power button, but nothing happened. He slid the phone into his pocket.

This was why she hadn't answered his phone calls. Who had done this? Who was out here with her? Was it Gravois? That seemed to be the only answer given her text message to Nick.

"Sarah!" He yelled her name as loud as he could. His heart ached as all kinds of possibilities raced through his head. Where could she be?

"Sarah," he yelled once again.

"Nick… Nick, help me." Her voice came from someplace deeper in the swamp.

He released a deep gasp of relief. She was alive!

But she was definitely in danger. He raced toward the sound of her voice, desperate to get to her.

"Sarah, I'm coming…keep yelling to me," he shouted.

"Nick…hurry." Her voice was filled with a terror that torched a like emotion inside him. He had to get to her. Oh God, he needed to save her from whoever was after her.

He ran as fast as possible, batting back tree limbs and jumping over pools of water. Any fear he'd had about being in the swamp was gone, replaced by his need to find the woman he loved.

He stopped for a brief moment, panting for air, and then he called her name again. There was no response. "Sarah," he cried, needing to hear her to find her in the vast vegetation.

She screamed, a blood-curdling sound that shot icy chills through him. "Sarah," he cried desperately. There was no reply. "Sarah?" he called her name over and over again as he hurried forward.

Oh God, why wasn't she answering? And what had made her scream like that? Frantically he ran. His biggest fear was that she was now in the clutches of the Honey Island Swamp Monster murderer.

He didn't know how long he continued to search, but without her calling to him it was futile. Was she still here in the swamp? Maybe. He just didn't know what to believe.

Gravois called me and I'm here just waiting for you and him to show up. Tonight, we get him!

He read her text again. Gravois. He had to be the killer and he'd lured Sarah here to make her his next victim. It didn't matter that she didn't fit his usual profile. The proof was in the text she'd sent to him. Gravois had called her and lured her out here.

Gravois. The man's name pounded over and over again in Nick's head. He needed to find the lawman as quickly as possible.

With this thought in mind, Nick ran to exit the swamp. There was nothing more he could do here by himself. The marshland was simply too big for him to find her by himself.

He finally reached Vincent's parking lot where Sarah's vehicle was still parked. He got into his car and leaned his forehead against the steering wheel, for a moment overwhelmed with emotion. Tears burned hot at his eyes and his chest tightened as a deep sob escaped him.

His love for Sarah ached inside him. He needed his partner. Was it already too late? No, he refused to believe that. It couldn't be too late. With this thought in mind, he swiped the tears out of his eyes, put the car into drive and tore out of the parking lot.

Hell, he didn't even know where Gravois lived. He'd have to go to the station and see if somebody there knew. He drove as fast as possible, aware that time was of the essence.

He pulled to a halt in front of the police station and went in the front door where Judd Lynons was on the front desk. "Hey, man, do you know Gravois's address?" Nick asked.

"Why? What's going on?" Judd asked curiously.

"I just need his address. It's important," Nick replied. He didn't want to waste time by explaining everything.

"I don't know his exact address, but I know he lives on Tupelo Lane. Tupelo Lane is off Main Street by Mike's Grocery store. His house is in the middle of the block. It's a blue two-story and…"

Nick didn't wait to hear anything more. He turned on his heels and then raced back outside to his car. He tore away from the curb and headed down Main Street where he knew the grocery store was located.

He gripped the steering wheel tightly as tears once again blurred his vision. *Please let her still be alive. Please let her still be alive.* The words repeated over and over again in his head. It was a mantra… a prayer that went around and around in his brain.

He reached the grocery store and saw Tupelo Lane. He made the left onto the street. Tall trees encroached on the narrow street as Nick drove slowly, checking the houses on either side of the road.

The neighborhood was old, but the houses appeared well-kept. And then he saw it. The house was a slate blue with a wraparound porch, and Gravois's official car was in the driveway.

He parked along the curb and his heart thundered as he got out of the car and raced to the front door. He knocked. There was no response. He knocked again, this time loud enough to wake the entire neighborhood.

"Hang on," Gravois's voice drifted out. After only a moment he opened the door. The man was without a shirt and was clad only in a pair of sleep pants. His hair was disheveled as if he'd just been pulled from his bed.

"Nick, what in the hell is going on?" he asked.

Nick stared at the man in confusion. This was not the Gravois that he'd expected to find. "Sarah is missing," he said.

Gravois frowned. "Missing? What do you mean she's missing? Isn't she at home? It's the middle of the night."

"No, she isn't home. She said you called her and told her to go to the swamp?"

Gravois's frown deepened and he stepped out of his door onto the porch with Nick. "I didn't call Sarah. The last time I spoke to her was this morning at the station. So what's going on here?"

"I don't know, but this is what I do know. Sarah was in the swamp." Nick went on to explain as quickly as possible everything that had happened when he'd arrived at the swamp.

"Dammit, if somebody has harmed Sarah, there will be hell to pay," Gravois said angrily. "I'll meet you at the station in fifteen minutes. I'll call in all the men and we'll search the swamp until we find her."

"I'll be at the station waiting for you," Nick replied, and then he got back into his car. As he headed back to the station his brain whirled. Did he believe Gravois? Yeah, he tended to believe him. He'd certainly reacted in a way that made Nick want to believe him. If he didn't believe Gravois was responsible, then who was?

Who had called Sarah and impersonated Gravois? Had she been too sleepy when she'd answered the phone to know that it wasn't Gravois? Was the call so short that somebody had fooled her? He supposed that was certainly a possibility.

So, who was it? Who had lured Sarah to the swamp? He believed it was the Honey Island Swamp Monster murderer. Sarah had believed she was too unimportant in the investigation for anyone to come after her, but somebody had definitely seen her as a threat.

By the time he reached the station, he was once again overwhelmed by a wealth of emotion. He went back into the little room he and Sarah had shared and sank down at the table to wait for Gravois to arrive.

Her scent was everywhere, that fresh floral fragrance that he found so attractive. He thought of her bright smile, the one that always made him feel like the sunshine was in his chest. She couldn't be dead. She had to be still alive. He needed her.

He jumped up out of the chair when he heard Gravois's voice booming down the hallway. He met the lawman in the hall. "I've called in all the men. The only one I couldn't get hold of was Ryan, but I left him a message to meet us at the swamp and that's where all the other men will meet us, so we need to head out."

"I'm right behind you," Nick replied, a new urgency filling his soul.

Twenty minutes later the men were all at Vincent's. All of them carried high-powered flashlights. It was impossible to do a normal grid search so Gravois appointed the men areas to go. Right now, it was a search-and-rescue operation. He hoped like hell it didn't change to become a recover maneuver.

He hurried to the place where he'd last heard her voice. Right now, the swamp was alive with the sounds of all the officers calling out her name.

Her name resonated in his heart, deep in his very soul. They had to find her and they had to find her alive. He continued to crash through the marsh, looking everywhere for her.

"Mr. Nick." Gator stepped out of the brush, nearly scaring Nick half to death. "What's going on here?"

"Gator, Sarah has gone missing and I last heard from her here in the swamp." Nick quickly explained what had happened. "Did you hear anything out here tonight? Did you see anything?"

"Most nights I'm out and about, but tonight I slept until I heard all the commotion, so the answer is no. I'm sorry, but I didn't see or hear anything. I'll help the search now."

"Thanks, Gator," Nick replied.

The old man nodded at him and then disappeared back into the brush and Nick continued moving forward. One more person searching could only help.

They searched until dawn when Gravois called things off because the men needed a break. They all agreed to reconvene at the station in a half an hour for more instructions.

Nick remained in Vincent's parking lot after the others had left. The morning sun was sparking on the trees, turning it all a rich golden color.

She wasn't there. His gut instinct told him she was no longer in the swamp. The search had been far-reaching, but the swamp was vast. But he now believed she'd been taken away from the swamp.

Had she been taken to the killing grounds? Where was that? How long did the killer keep his victims there before killing them? Maybe minutes…hopefully hours.

Once again, a wealth of emotion tightened his chest and tears blurred his vision. Where was Sarah? If what he believed was true, then one of the cops who had helped search for her was the same person who had taken her.

And where was Ryan? He hadn't shown up for the search. Suddenly it was imperative that he find Ryan.

Chapter Twelve

Sarah regained consciousness slowly. The first thing she noticed was the huge headache that stretched painfully across her forehead. She tried to open her eyes, but she was still too groggy and it felt as if her eyelids weighed a thousand pounds.

She remained still and simply breathed, but there was a noxious smell surrounding her. It was horrible and it reminded her of the stench in James Noman's shanty. Oh God, is that where she was?

No…that wasn't right. Her brain began to slowly clear. She'd gotten a call from Gravois and she'd gone to the swamp. Her smashed phone and the race through the swamp…all the events of the night suddenly flashed in her head.

Gravois. Dear God, it had been him all along. He was the Honey Island Swamp Monster killer. She'd run so hard and so fast last night to escape him and the hypodermic needle he'd held in his hand.

When she'd heard Nick, she'd hoped…she'd prayed he would get to her before Gravois did, but that hadn't happened. If she hadn't tripped over a big tuber, she might have escaped him. But the moment she hit the ground he was on her.

She screamed and fought with him, but ultimately, he'd managed to get the needle in her arm. She'd continued to fight for several more moments before darkness had gripped her and she knew no more.

So where was she now? She finally managed to open her eyes. She was tied to a straight-backed chair and appeared to be in a basement. Even though there were few basements in the area, there were some. This wasn't just any basement; she knew she was in the killing ground.

Oh God. Dried blood stained the floor all around her chair. The stench was so horrendous and she knew it came from what was left of the poor victims. This was where Gravois not only stabbed the women, but also where he ripped out their throats and tore off their faces.

She had to get out. She struggled against the ropes that held her arms behind her as gasping cries escaped her. She twisted and turned her wrists. If she could just get one hand out of the ropes, she would be able to untie herself and escape.

There were no sounds from the upstairs and she sensed she was alone in whatever place she was at. Was the basement in Gravois's house? It had been years since she'd been inside his home.

She continued to fight to get free, but there was

no give in the ropes. She fought until she was out of breath and gasping with pain and sheer terror. How long would it be before Gravois would come back here?

She finally leaned her head back and sobbed. Nobody would know that the chief of police was the monster. Except Nick. If he got her text then he should know.

So why wasn't he here? Did her text not go through? You couldn't always depend on technology. If for some reason he hadn't gotten her text then nobody would know she was here. Nobody would ever suspect the chief of police. She'd even assured Nick that there was no way she'd believe that Gravois was responsible for the murders. She'd been wrong…so very wrong.

Right now, she was on her own. Somehow, someway, she had to get out of here. She drew in several deep breaths and then began working her hands once again, twisting and turning them until she was once again crying and her wrists felt raw enough to be bleeding.

It took several minutes for her to calm herself. She had to stay calm so she could think rationally. She did not want to become another victim of the Honey Island Swamp Monster murderer.

For the first time she began to look around the room. In front of her was a small wooden workbench with two deep drawers, but there was nothing on top of it. However hanging above it was a gardening claw. The tool looked dirty with rust-colored stains she believed to be blood.

Was that what he used to tear out his victim's throats? To rake their faces off? She swallowed hard against the new wave of emotions that rose up inside her. It wasn't just terror; it was also abject horror that filled her.

This felt like a scene from a horrible horror film, one of those sick, bloody films that she had always refused to watch. And now she was living it.

To her left was a staircase leading up and to her right...dear heavens...there was an old red recliner chair and in the chair was an intact human skeleton.

Gravois's missing wife. The one who had supposedly left him years ago. Yvette. She hadn't left at all. She'd been murdered and her body had been here all along.

For the first time since she'd opened her eyes, Sarah screamed.

THANKFULLY GRAVOIS WAS at the station when Nick arrived. Nick immediately went into his office. "We need to check out Ryan. He didn't show up for the search and he could be our man."

"You're right. With all the commotion going on, I didn't miss him being there, but it's very suspicious that he didn't show up at all."

"Where does he live?"

"He has a little house just outside the city limits.

I'll gather up a couple of men and we'll head there right now." Gravois got up from his desk and twenty minutes later Nick was following behind his car to Ryan's place.

The man had brought them no alibis for the nights of the murders and he'd been no place to be found when Sarah had disappeared. Nick also hadn't realized the man lived in a house just out of the city limits. A house that might hold the killing grounds. A man who possibly had Sarah right now.

The tiredness from the all-night search disappeared as a new burst of adrenaline filled Nick. This had to be it, and he prayed that they weren't already too late. The last thing he wanted to do was find Sarah's body, her throat torn out and her beautiful face ravaged, behind some random building in town.

At least Gravois drove fast as if filled with the same anxious energy Nick felt. Behind Nick were two more patrol cars, each carrying two officers.

They finally pulled up in Ryan's long driveway. The house was small, probably a two-bedroom. There was also a detached garage. Ryan's vehicle was in the drive, indicating that he was home.

Gravois took the lead, marching up to the front door and knocking. He waited a moment and then knocked again more forcefully.

"Officer Staub," he yelled.

"Yeah...yeah, I'm coming," Ryan yelled. A moment later he opened his door. The man looked like hell. He was clad in a pair of sleep pants and a gray T-shirt. His face was unusually pale and he looked at them all in confusion.

"What's going on? I'm sorry I missed the search but I'm sick as a dog," he said. "I've got a temperature of 102 and I've been throwing up my guts for most of the night and day, so why are you all here?"

"We're still looking for Sarah," Nick said. "Mind if we come in?"

Ryan looked at him in surprise. "You think Sarah is in here? You really think I'm the killer?" He opened his door wide to allow them entry. "It's not me, man. You're all wasting your time here."

"Check out the garage," Gravois said to the other men and then he and Nick stepped into the house.

There was a blue sheet on the sofa and a box of tissues and a bottle of cold medicine on the coffee table. There was no nasty scent to indicate anything nefarious had happened in here.

"Feel free to look around," Ryan said as he sank back down on the sofa. "I can't even believe you all think I'd have anything to do with the murders or whatever happened to Sarah. I would never, ever hurt that woman."

They did look around. Gravois went into the kitchen while Nick looked in each of the two bedrooms. There was nothing suspicious anywhere in the house. The other officers returned from outside and shook their heads, indicating there was nothing in the garage.

Bitter disappointment shot through Nick. She wasn't here, so where was she? They all agreed to meet back at the station in a half an hour or so. Once there, they would try to figure out where to go from here.

Nick returned to the station and sat in their little room, a sickness filling his soul. So much time had passed since he'd heard her cries in the swamp. If she was still alive, he knew time was running out for her.

Frantically, he went over all the notes they'd made that day, looking for something that would jump out at him.

He was so afraid. His childhood trauma, snakes beneath the bed and the gunfire in the parking lot... none of that had prepared him for the kind of fear that torched through him now.

He'd made her promise to carry on if anything happened to him, but he'd never seen the danger that was coming after her. Why in the hell hadn't he realized that she was at risk?

His job had been to come in and solve this case. He'd told her he'd never lost a partner before but she was so much more than his partner.

Now he didn't know where she was and his heart was slowly dying.

SARAH HAD FOUGHT against the ropes for what felt like hours...days, and she still found no give in them. She'd fought as hard as she could and had wept all her tears she had inside her.

She now leaned her head forward and began to feel a weary acceptance. She was going to die at the hands of the man she'd believed had loved her as a daughter. She was going to die here in this chamber of horrors.

Why, in all the years she'd known him, hadn't she seen the darkness that must be in his soul? Why had she never seen the utter evil that resided inside him?

Thank God, she hadn't burdened Nick by telling him how much she loved him. Hopefully he would go on with the investigation and he'd eventually get Gravois behind bars.

That didn't stop her from mourning what might have been. Even if things hadn't worked out with Nick, she'd still wanted to be somebody's wife. She'd wanted babies to fill her arms and to build a real family with some special man. She hadn't realized how badly she'd wanted that, and she had wanted that with Nick. Now she would never get any of those opportunities.

At least with her death she would be reunited with her parents in heaven. She'd once again be with the two people who had loved her unconditionally and had been her best friends.

A vision of Nick filled her head. His handsome features were ingrained in her brain, along with the sound of his deep, wonderful laughter. She loved the way his forehead wrinkled when he was deep in concentration and the way his smile warmed her throughout. She loved everything about him and she just wished she would have had an opportunity to tell him goodbye.

She straightened up as she heard the sound of a door opening and then closing from upstairs. It had to be Gravois and he was probably here for one reason…to stab her and then rip out her throat and tear off her face.

Once again, she began struggling against the ropes, sheer panic coursing through her. The door at the top of the stairs opened and she began to cry.

Gravois's heavy footsteps coming down the stairs sounded like the rhythm of death coming for her. Then he stood before her.

"Ah, Sarah, I'm so sorry it's come to this," he said with pity in his voice. "Unfortunately, your boyfriend seems to have angel wings of protection around him. The snakes didn't kill him nor was I able to shoot him to death. But I'm sure your death will mess with his mind so much he'll have to quit the investigation."

"He'll never stop. He's going to throw you in jail, Gravois," she said angrily. "You'll suffer for the rest of your life in prison. I can't believe you killed all those young women. I can't believe you're such a monster. And…and is that Yvette?"

"It is my lovely Yvette." His features softened as he gazed at the skeleton in the chair. "It's been years now, but we had a fight and I pushed her. She fell over and hit her head on the edge of the coffee table. Unfortunately, it was a fatal blow. My beautiful, loving wife died."

"Why didn't you go to the authorities? If it was an accident then you wouldn't have been in any trouble," she replied. She needed to keep him talking, on the off chance somebody would find her…that somebody could save her.

"For God's sake, Gravois, why not at least give her a proper burial?" she asked.

"I didn't want anyone taking her away from me," he replied, his voice raised and his eyes slightly wild. "I love her more than anyone on the face of the planet and I needed her here with me. I needed to keep her here with me. I'll love her until the day I die."

"So, why kill all the women from the swamp?" Sarah asked softly, trying to calm him.

"Yvette looked like a lot of the women from the swamp. She had the same beautiful features as the swamp women. I just needed to find the right face. If I found the right one, then I would be able to give Yvette a face back."

Sarah stared at him in true revulsion. This was something out of the worst horror movie. "Gravois, you need help." He was obviously horribly mentally ill. To think that he was hunting for a face to give to his dead wife…the thought shuddered inside her.

"I don't need help," he yelled, his face turning red. "I just need to find the right damn face. So far, they've been all wrong. When I got them back here, I realized their faces were all wrong, so I erased them."

He stalked over to the workbench and opened one of the drawers. He withdrew a sharp-looking knife and then turned back to face her.

"Gravois, you don't want to do this," she cried frantically. "Please, you don't have to kill me. Let me go and I won't tell anyone about this. I'll make sure I screw up the investigation so nobody will ever come after you."

"Ah, sweet Sarah, you're just lying to me now."

"I'm not… I'm not lying to you," she replied fervently. She would say anything to him just to get him to let her go unharmed. "Gravois, please, you can trust me."

He shook his head. "I would never trust you. You've become a good cop, Sarah, and good cops want to get the bad guys off the streets. You're definitely a threat to what I'm trying to accomplish here."

"But I have loyalty toward you. You helped me so much after my parents died. You were there for me, Gravois, and I haven't forgotten that. Now I want to be here for you."

He laughed, but there was no humor in the laughter. Instead, it was a sick, twisted sound. "You're good, Sarah. You're very good. But nothing you say is going to stop what's about to happen."

He jabbed the knife forward. "I'm sorry that the first couple of stabs are going to hurt you, but hopefully you won't be conscious when I rip out your throat and tear your face off."

He stabbed the knife into her stomach and she screamed as excruciating pain ripped through her and she realized she was definitely the next victim of the Honey Island Swamp Monster murderer.

NICK SAT IN the room and went over all their notes and picked apart everything that had happened. Somewhere in the minutiae of it all, he had made a mistake or overlooked something important. He thought about everything that had happened since the moment he'd received the notification from Sarah on his phone.

The notification had said that Gravois had called her yet the man had denied that had happened. When Nick had gone to Gravois's house, the man had looked disheveled and as if he'd just climbed out of bed. But how easy would it have been for him to tousle his hair and change into a pair of sleep pants?

He'd stepped outside his house to talk to Nick. Why hadn't he invited Nick inside? A headache pounded in Nick's head. Gravois, the name once again thundered in his head.

Why had he not investigated the cases better? Why had he partnered Nick with somebody who knew nothing about the cases? Where had Gravois been on the nights of the murders? And where was

Gravois now? Why would he call for a half an hour break in the search efforts?

God, Nick had been such a fool. He jumped up from the table and ran down the hallway to Gravois's office. He knocked once and then threw open the door. Gravois wasn't there.

A wild panic rose up in him. Gravois, it was the only thing that made sense. Dammit, Nick had suspected the man and now it was imperative that Nick get to his home and see if Sarah was there.

Colby Shanks and Ian Brubaker were standing by the dispatch desk. "Can you two come with me?" he asked urgently.

"Where?" they asked in unison.

"To Gravois's place. I think Sarah is there and I need you two to back me up."

"You think Gravois is the killer?" Shanks asked in shocked surprise.

"I do and I think Sarah is there and in danger. Will you come with me?"

The two officers looked at each other. "I'll go," Shanks said, and looked back at Nick.

"I definitely need to go, too," Brubaker agreed.

"Then let's go." Nick ran outside to his car, got in and tore out of the parking lot. All his nerves were electrified, shooting a fierce alarm through him. A glance in his rearview mirror showed him that the two officers were behind him.

Was it already too late? Oh God, how much of

a lead did Gravois have on him? Had the man had enough time to go home and kill Sarah?

Tears of fear and frustration filled Nick's eyes. It couldn't be too late. She couldn't be gone already. His heart beat so fast he felt as if it might explode right out of his chest.

He reached Tupelo Lane and turned left, cutting off another driver who honked at him and gave him the finger. Nick didn't care, he had to get to Gravois's place as quickly as possible.

He pulled into Gravois's driveway behind the lawman's car. He parked and flew out of the car. It was only when he reached the front door that a wave of doubts overcame him.

Was he jumping to conclusions? Was this just all a big mistake? No, it couldn't be. His gut instinct told him that this was right. Shanks and Brubaker joined him on the porch. Nick knocked hard on the door and it creaked open.

He immediately drew his gun. The minute he stepped into the house he knew for certain he was right. The faint odor of human blood and decay filled his nose.

The two officers followed right behind him. "Check the bedrooms," he said to them. While they disappeared down the hallway, Nick checked the living room and kitchen, but found nothing incriminating.

Where was the man? He had to be home. His car

was outside. Brubaker and Shanks walked into the living room. "Nothing," Shanks said.

"Gravois," Nick yelled.

"Nick! We're down here," Sarah called.

He nearly fell to his knees at the sound of her voice. She was alive! Down here? There must be a basement. He opened one door and found a closet.

He ran to the kitchen where there were two doors. He'd already checked them once. The first one was a pantry. The second appeared to be a broom closet, but now on closer inspection, Nick saw that it had a false back. He pulled it away and a staircase was revealed.

"Gravois," he shouted. "It's over, man. Don't hurt her." Nick took two steps down and bent over to see the situation. The stench down here was horrendous and as he perused the area, his blood ran cold.

She was tied in a chair and Gravois stood before her with a bloody knife in his hand. "Put the knife down," he yelled. "Put the knife down right now." He raced down the rest of the stairs and pointed his gun at Gravois. "If you don't put it down right now, I'm going to shoot you."

Gravois looked at him and in the man's eyes radiated the evil that was inside him. "Can you really shoot me before I stab her?" he taunted.

Nick fired. The bullet hit Gravois in the thigh and with a scream of pain the lawman went down to the ground. Nick kicked the knife out of his hand and across the floor. "Call for an ambulance and put him in cuffs," Nick said to the others.

He ran to Sarah's side. "It's okay, baby. You're safe now," he said. He left her only to look in the workbench drawer for something he could use to cut the ropes that held her. He found another knife there and hurried back to her side.

She was quietly crying as he worked the knife back and forth against the thick rope. As he labored, he gazed around the kill chamber, horrified by the skeleton that sat nearby in a chair.

He didn't know who the skeleton belonged to but eventually he would find out. It appeared it was another murder Gravois would be charged with. He continued to talk soothingly to Sarah as Gravois yelled his rage.

"Why didn't you just shoot me in the heart?" Gravois screamed.

"Because I want you alive to face all the disgust from your officers. I want you alive to waste away in prison," Nick said tersely.

"Damn you," Gravois yelled as Brubaker and Shanks got him in handcuffs.

"Nick..." Sarah said with a gasping breath.

"It's okay, honey. You're almost free now," he replied. He cut through the last of the rope and it fell not only from her hands but from her waist as well.

It was only then he saw it...the blood that covered

her stomach. "Sarah, oh God." He pulled up her shirt and saw the two gaping, bloody wounds in her belly.

"Nick," she whispered. Her eyes fluttered several times and then she fell unconscious.

"Get an ambulance here now," Nick cried. Had he been too late after all? Had Gravois mortally wounded Sarah? His heart cried out with anguish.

Chapter Thirteen

Nick sat in the waiting room in the emergency area of the hospital. The ambulance had finally arrived and Sarah was now in emergency surgery. She'd never regained consciousness while she'd been with Nick.

Once again, an abject fear coursed through him. He had no idea how badly she'd been hurt, how deep the stab wounds had been. But he couldn't help but remember the other victims had died from their stab wounds.

He'd been waiting for about an hour now to hear something, anything about her condition but so far nobody had come out to speak with him.

He knew Gravois was also here in the hospital getting surgery for his gunshot wound. He was also being guarded by Officers Kurby and Shanks.

Brubaker was the deputy police chief and he would be taking over the mess that Gravois had left behind until a special election could be held to appoint a new chief.

Brubaker would also be in charge of the crime

scene and collecting the evidence that would send Gravois away for the rest of his life. There was no question in Nick's mind that the blood of all the victims was in that basement.

He couldn't believe what a hellhole Sarah had been held in. He couldn't begin to imagine what kind of horror she must have felt when she saw that skeleton sitting in the chair. God, she must have been so afraid.

She had to be all right. Please, she had to survive this. She was a fighter, but could she fight for her life despite those knife wounds?

He leaned forward and dropped his head in his hands. *Please let her survive.* He couldn't imagine a world without her in it. The world needed that beautiful smile of hers.

The outer door whooshed open and he was surprised to see Ryan walk in. He looked better than he had earlier that morning. "My fever broke and I heard the news about Sarah," he said. He sank down two chairs away from Nick. "Have you heard anything?"

"Nothing," Nick replied.

"I can't believe it was Gravois all along," Ryan said.

"He's not only a serious danger, but he's also a disgrace to law enforcement," Nick said with disgust.

"This is certainly going to shake up this entire town," Ryan replied. "I wouldn't be surprised if this doesn't make national news, a police chief who is a serial killer. So, does this mean you'll be leaving soon?"

"Not for a week or so. I want to make sure we get all the evidence we need for the case. Don't worry, I'll be out of your hair soon and then the path will be clear for you with Sarah." Even saying those words shot an arrow of pain through Nick.

Ryan released a dry laugh. "There's no path forward for me with Sarah. In case you haven't noticed, she's totally in love with you."

Nick didn't reply. Ryan's words only made Nick's heart hurt more. "I appreciate you coming here," he finally said.

"Despite what it's looked like, I care about Sarah as a friend and coworker. I would never want this for her."

"You should see Gravois's basement," Nick replied, and then described the utter madness to Ryan.

"I can't imagine how Sarah felt trapped there," Ryan replied.

"I just wonder what's taking so long? Why hasn't the doctor come out to talk to me yet?" Nick said in frustration.

Was it a good sign or a bad sign that it was taking so long? Was she still in surgery or had she succumbed to her wounds?

Fifteen minutes later a tall, dark-haired man came into the room. Both Nick and Ryan jumped to their feet. "Mr. Cain, I'm Dr. Etienne Richards," he said.

"How's Sarah?" Nick asked as his heart pounded with an unsteady rhythm.

"Given no complications, she should be fine. Unfortunately, one of the knife wounds caught her gallbladder so I had to remove it and I also had to do some muscle repair. Her wrists are raw but right now she's in stable condition."

"Can I see her?" Nick asked.

The doctor shook his head negatively. "She's sleeping now and I intend to keep her comfortable with pain medicine for the rest of the day. It would be better to come back and visit with her tomorrow."

Nick was disappointed but wasn't about to argue. "Thank you, Dr. Richards," he said. The doctor nodded at both of them and then went back through the door.

"At least we know she's going to be okay," Ryan said. "And now I'm dragging myself back to my sofa. See you later, Nick." Ryan left the waiting room.

Nick left as well. It was time to work the crime scene. He got in his car and headed back to Gravois's house. As he drove his heart was filled with wild relief. She had survived her time with a serial killer. Thank God, she was going to be okay.

Now he needed to do his job to ensure that all the evidence was photographed and collected. Everything had to be done by the book so there was no way Gravois would be freed on a technicality.

When he pulled up out front of the blue house on Tupelo Lane there were three patrol cars there plus a hearse, which indicated the coroner was also there.

As Nick reached the front door, Officer Ken Mayfield and the coroner's assistant carried up a stretcher with the skeleton on top. Dr. Cartwright followed after them.

"Hell of a day," he said to Nick. "Is Sarah okay?"

"She had to go through surgery, but at the moment she's stable," Nick replied.

"Good, at least she's better than that poor woman," he said, and pointed to the skeleton that was being carried to the hearse. "Who knew that Gravois was so sick. He had to have been sick to keep that and to kill all those young women." He shook his head. "Hell of a day," he repeated. "I'll talk to you later." He headed toward the hearse.

Nick went into the house and down the stairs where Brubaker appeared to have a good handle on things. There were three other officers with him and two of them were collecting blood samples around the chair while the other officer was standing by.

"Hey, Nick, what's the word on Sarah?" Brubaker asked.

Nick told him the same thing he'd told Dr. Cartwright. "How can I help?"

"I think we've got it covered right now. We've already taken the crime scene photos and collected both the knife and a claw gardening tool. We'll probably be here for the rest of the day collecting the evidence that hopefully will tie him to all the Swamp Monster murders."

Brubaker shook his head. "I can't believe he was responsible for all the carnage. He was a man I looked up to, the man I worked closely with. Damn, but I'm so disgusted right now, both with him and with myself for not seeing the evil in him."

Nick clapped Brubaker on the shoulder. "Don't beat yourself up. Nobody saw him for what he was. A lot of responsibility just fell on your shoulders. I have confidence that when I leave here the department will be in good hands."

"Thanks. I really appreciate that coming from you."

"If you don't mind, I'll just hang out here awhile and if you need me just tell me what to do," Nick replied.

"That would be great," Brubaker replied. "The problem is this is a relatively small space so not many people can work it. Right now, those two are getting what we need." He gestured to the two officers taking blood samples.

Nick took a seat on the stairs and he remained there until dinnertime. He missed Sarah. While he wouldn't want her down here in the stench and the memories of being tied up, he wished she was here by his side.

He missed the scent of her perfume surrounding

him, her leaning over to whisper something in his ear. At least he could see her tomorrow, although he didn't know how long she'd be in the hospital.

As much as he missed her today, it wouldn't be long before he would leave Black Bayou and Sarah behind. He'd leave his heart here with her and it would take a very long time to get over her.

But he had to leave her. The worst thing he could do was allow her to continue loving him. She would eventually want marriage and he knew what kind of a husband he was.

She deserved a terrific husband in her life and so the kindest thing he could do was let her go.

SARAH AWOKE AND for a moment didn't know where she was. She started to jerk up but then pain tore through her stomach. She looked around and realized she was in the hospital. Evening light cast in through the window and she was alone in the room.

She relaxed back and tried to process how she had gotten here. The last thing she remembered was being tied up in Gravois's basement as he stabbed her. She reached down and touched her stomach, which had bandages across it.

Then she remembered Nick coming down the stairs. Nick. He'd found her. He'd shot Gravois and saved her very life. Her love for him blossomed in her chest, filling it with a delicious warmth.

Somehow, she'd been brought here and whatever

the doctor had done for her, it had obviously saved her life as well. She needed to know what had been done to her. Would she still be able to have children, or had Gravois taken that away from her with his knife wounds?

She looked around until she found a call button and then she pushed it, hoping whoever answered would be able to give her some information.

Moments later a nurse came in and introduced herself as Kelly. "I know Dr. Richards has been waiting for you to wake up. I'll just go get him now."

"Thank you," Sarah replied, and raised the head of her bed.

"How's my patient?" Dr. Richards asked as he came into the room a few minutes later.

"I'm having some pain, but what I want right now is some information."

As she listened to what the doctor had done, a wave of relief rushed through her. Who needed a gallbladder anyway? At least there had been no other real damage to her.

"Before you go, Dr. Richards, have you seen my partner, Nick?"

"He was here earlier and wanted to see you, but I told him it would be better if he came back tomorrow to visit with you."

"Okay, thank you," she replied.

"I'll see that the nurse gets you some more pain meds and I'll see you in the morning as well." Dr.

Richards left and the nurse came in and administered the pain medication.

It wasn't long before Sarah drifted back off to sleep. She awakened with the morning sun streaming brightness into the room. Her stomach was sore but she knew it was going to take some time for her to heal.

She raised the head of her bed and wondered when Nick would be in to see her. The crime was now solved and so there was nothing more keeping him here. He would be leaving her any day now.

Unless…unless her words of love for him would keep him with her. She was running out of time. She had to talk to him today and tell him how much she loved him. Along with the ache in her stomach, her nerves formed a wave of anxiety as she anticipated laying her heart out on the line to him.

She hadn't been awake long when breakfast arrived. Breakfast consisted of coffee, broth and gelatin. She immediately took off the lid to the coffee and sipped on it. She hoped when they dismissed her, she would be armed with information about diet after gallbladder removal. Hopefully it wouldn't be broth and gelatin for the rest of her life.

She wound up drinking all the broth and eating the gelatin, then continued to sip on her coffee as thoughts of Nick swirled around in her head.

Her breakfast tray had just been removed when

Dr. Richards came into the room. "Sarah, how are you doing this morning?"

"Better than last time I spoke with you," she replied.

"That's always what a doctor wants to hear."

"I do have more questions for you this morning."

"Hopefully I have answers for you," he replied.

She asked him about recovery time, surprised when he told her six to eight weeks. Then she questioned him about diet and finally she asked when she could be released from the hospital. Without any complications, she could go home in two to three days.

Once the doctor left, she turned on her television to pass the time. She was halfway through a game show when he walked in. As always, Nick looked handsome clad in black slacks and a gray polo that perfectly matched his eyes. His familiar scent smelled like safety…like home.

"Sarah," he said softly as he sat in the chair next to her and reached for her hand.

All the trauma she'd been through suddenly rose up inside her and she began to cry. "Oh, honey… don't do that. It will only make you hurt more."

"Oh, Nick, it…it was so horrible," she choked out amid her tears. "Being in—in that basement wi-with so much death surrounding me. And—and then Gravois there with a knife. I—I was so sure I was going to die down there."

"But you didn't," he replied gently.

"Thanks to you." She managed to get her crying under control as she squeezed his hand tightly. "How did you know it was Gravois?"

She listened as he told her everything that had happened after she'd disappeared from the swamp. "Thank God, you sent me that text, but Gravois was a crafty one and initially fooled me."

They continued to talk about the case for the next half an hour or so. "You look tired," she observed. His features were slightly drawn with what looked like exhaustion.

"I was up most of the night helping the men collect all the evidence at Gravois's house," he replied.

"He needs mental help. He told me the skeleton was his wife and he was taking the swamp women hoping he could somehow take their face to put on her. But each time he got them to his basement he realized their faces were all wrong. He's definitely mentally ill."

"I doubt he'll get much help in prison, and that's where he belongs," Nick replied. "The good thing is it's finally over. The bad guy is behind bars and according to what the doctor told me you're going to be just fine."

"I'm not going to be fine, Nick. I'm so deeply in love with you. I won't be fine without you," she said. She watched him closely and felt the press of tears once again burning in her eyes as his turned a cold dark, slate gray.

"I want to marry you and give you babies. I want to spend the rest of my life with you. Please, Nick. I know you love me, too," she babbled. Why were his eyes so emotionless while she felt herself falling completely apart?

"Sarah." He pulled his hand from hers. "You knew going into this that eventually I'd go home. I never promised you anything. I even told you I'm not husband material."

"But you are," she protested. "Maybe you and your ex-wife weren't right for each other, but we are, Nick. Look into my eyes, Nick, and tell me you don't love me." She held his gaze, looking for a softening, and she gasped with relief as she saw it.

"That doesn't matter, Sarah. Even if I do love you, I don't intend to do anything about it. I'm sorry, Sarah, but in a couple of days I'll be going home and hopefully in time you'll find the perfect man for you here in Black Bayou."

She stared at him as he stood. How could he not see they were perfect for each other? "Have you ever considered that your ex-wife was wrong about you? You couldn't have been a lousy husband, Nick, because you're not a lousy man. You're the man I choose. I don't want anyone else but you."

"I'm so sorry, Sarah. It was never my intention to hurt you. I'll check in with you before I leave town and now, I'll just let you rest." With that, he left her room.

Rest? Her heart had just been ripped out of her very body. A rush of tears overwhelmed her and she began to cry in earnest. She'd been so hopeful, so sure that he loved her as much as she did him.

She'd been filled with such dreams of the two of them together. She'd been so sure they would have a life together and now all those dreams had been destroyed.

She didn't know how long she wept. By the time she pulled herself together Ryan and Judd Lynons walked in carrying a large vase of flowers.

For the rest of the afternoon officers came in carrying flowers and plants and good wishes. There was definitely a new respect in the way they interacted with her. At least she'd gained that, but nothing could warm her heart with the loss of Nick so fresh.

By the end of the day her room looked like a floral shop and all the officers had been in to visit with her. She directed the nurse to disperse some of the flowers to other hospital rooms.

As the darkness of night fell, so did more tears. She wept until she could weep no more. She'd been so excited to tell Nick how she felt and in her heart of hearts, she'd thought he'd sweep her up in his arms and tell her how much he loved her, how much he wanted to spend the rest of his life with her. Now she just felt empty, so achingly empty.

Over the next three days the emptiness was filled with heartache as she continued to mourn the loss of her dreams…the loss of Nick. She kept hoping he would come back in and tell her he couldn't live without her after all, and that he wanted a life with her. But that hadn't happened.

She was finally released from the hospital and Ryan drove her home. She'd been settled in at home for two days when a knock fell on her door. She went to answer and found Nick on her doorstep.

She hadn't heard from or seen him since he'd walked out of her hospital room and taken her heart with him. She opened her door and gestured him in. As he swept past her, she smelled that familiar scent of him, a scent that now only brought her more pain.

"Hi, Sarah." He stopped just inside the door. "I told you I'd stop by on my way out of town."

"So, you're leaving," she replied. Her heart began a new dull ache of loss.

"I am. I'll probably have to come back a couple of times as it relates to the prosecution of Gravois, but for right now I guess this is goodbye." He oozed discomfort as he gazed at her.

She wasn't going to let him off the hook so easily. "You were an excellent partner. You taught me so much and I loved the time we spent together."

"We were good partners," he agreed.

"We could still be good partners in life," she said softly. "Oh, Nick, if you'd just look deep within your heart, I know you'll find the kind of love for me that will last us a lifetime. All you have to do is take a chance on me, take a chance on us."

His eyes darkened. "I'm sorry that I can't give you what you want, Sarah," he replied with regret rife in his tone.

"I hate your ex-wife," she replied suddenly. He looked at her in surprise. "I hate her because I think she made you believe things about yourself that aren't true, things that have destroyed your ability to believe in yourself, to know what kind of a good man you are. Trust me, Nick. Don't trust her."

"Sarah, I just came by to tell you goodbye." He edged back toward the door.

"I love you, Nick," she said one last time, knowing once he walked out of the door, she would never see him again.

He hesitated for a long moment and in that moment, she held her breath, hoping...praying that she'd finally reached him. "Goodbye, Sarah," he finally said, and then walked out the door.

She wanted to run after him and throw her arms around him. She wanted to beg him to reconsider, but she did have a little bit of pride left. She sank down on her sofa, her heart pain too deep for even tears at this moment.

What would be the point of chasing after him? He knew how she felt and he'd rejected her anyway. Twice he'd rejected her. There was no more she could say to him. Now she had to figure out how to live without him.

Three weeks passed and physically she was feeling pretty much back to normal. But there wasn't a minute that went by that she didn't miss Nick. She had so many memories of him burned deep in her heart and she couldn't forget them.

She had been off work on sick leave and the house echoed around her with emptiness. Her loneliness was intense but she knew nobody else would assuage it except the man who had been her partner.

Hopefully, when she did return to work Brubaker would assign her to some serious case or another so she could immerse herself in something other than missing Nick. Hopefully Brubaker would see her for the good police officer she'd become.

It was right after noon on the twenty-third day since she'd last seen Nick and she'd just made herself a sandwich for lunch when there was a knock on her door.

She left her lunch and went to the door. She gasped in stunned surprise as she saw Nick.

What was he doing back here? Did he need something as far as the case was concerned? Weeks ago, she had given Brubaker her official statement about her time with Gravois. What could Nick need from her?

For a moment she wished she were dressed in something other than a slightly faded pink T-shirt and a pair of gray jogging pants. He looked amazing in a pair of jeans and a white long-sleeved dress shirt.

She put up all her defenses as she opened the door. "Hi, Sarah, can I come in?" he asked.

Silently she ushered him in. He went directly into her living room and sank down on the sofa.

"What are you doing here, Nick?" she asked as her heart beat an unsteady rhythm. She didn't sit, but rather remained standing. She didn't want to be close enough to him to smell his cologne or allow him to touch her in any way.

"How are you feeling?" he asked.

"As good as new," she replied. Did he have any idea what his presence here was doing to her? As much as she wanted to be strong and unaffected by him, her love for him still burned deep inside her heart and soul. "Why are you here? I'm sure you didn't travel here just to ask me how I'm doing."

"Actually, I was hoping you could help me solve a case."

She frowned at him. "What kind of case?" Had he lost his mind? Why would he be back here in Black Bay asking her about a case?

"It's about a missing woman. I've realized over the past three weeks that I need her in my life. She's a woman I want to desperately find because she fulfills me in a way I never expected." He stood, his gaze soft and warm on her. "Oh, Sarah, I've been such a fool."

She took a step toward him, her heart thundering in her chest. Was this for real? Was he really here for her? She was so afraid to believe it.

"But there's more," he said, stopping her in her tracks. "The woman has to be willing to relocate for me. The bad news is she'll need to leave everything here behind, but the good news is the New Orleans Police Department is always looking for good officers and if that's what she wants she'll easily be able to get a job."

He took a step toward her, his gaze so soft…so loving. "Sarah, I love you so much and I can't imagine you not being in my life. The last three weeks without you have been absolute hell. Marry me, Sarah, and I promise I will try to be the very best husband you would ever want. Marry me and make me the happiest man in the world."

"Are you sure, Nick?" she asked, her heart on the verge of exploding with happiness.

"I've never been so sure in my entire life," he replied.

She could stand it no longer. She flew into his arms where he wrapped his arms around her and kissed her long and deep. When the kiss ended, he stared down at her intently.

"Are you sure you're willing to relocate? I mean, you have a house here and ties to your friends," he said.

"I can sell my house and honestly, Nick, this has never really felt like home. I found home with you and yes, I'm more than willing to relocate," she replied.

He laughed. "I guess Nene was right about me after all," he said.

She looked up at him curiously. "Why? What did she say about you?"

"On the first day I arrived here she told me that I was like one of the heroes in the romance books she read. I was the handsome stranger who had come to save the day and, in the process, would find my own true love." He grinned down at her. "Funny how right she was."

"Funny how right you were to come and get me. You are my hero, Nick, and I will always love you," she replied.

"And I will always, always love you," he replied.

He took her lips once again in a kiss that whispered of passion but screamed of love. Even though she hadn't been looking for love, Nick had come into her life and everything had changed for her. She was truly home with him and she knew their partnership was going to last a lifetime.

* * * * *

COMING NEXT MONTH FROM

HARLEQUIN

INTRIGUE

#2205 BIG SKY DECEPTION

Silver Stars of Montana • by BJ Daniels

Sheriff Brandt Parker knows that nothing short of her father's death could have lured Molly Lockhart to Montana. He's determined to protect the stubborn, independent woman but keeping his own feelings under control is an additional challenge as his investigation unfolds.

#2206 WHISPERING WINDS WIDOWS

Lookout Mountain Mysteries • by Debra Webb

Lucinda was angry when her husband left his job in the city to work with his father. Deidre never shared her husband's dream of moving to Nashville. And Harlowe wanted a baby that her husband couldn't give her. When their men vanished, the Whispering Winds Widows told the same story. Will the son of one of the disappeared and a writer from Chattanooga finally uncover the truth?

#2207 K-9 SHIELD

New Mexico Guard Dogs • by Nichole Severn

Jones Driscoll has spent half his life in war zones. This rescue mission feels different. Undercover journalist Maggie Caddel is tough—and yet she still rouses his instinct to protect. She might trust him to help her bring down the cartel that held her captive, but neither of them has any reason to let down their guards and trust the connection they share.

#2208 COLD MURDER IN KOLTON LAKE

The Lynleys of Law Enforcement • by R. Barri Flowers

Reviewing a cold case, FBI special agent Scott Lynley needs the last person to see the victim alive. Still haunted by her aunt's death, FBI victim specialist Abby Zhang is eager to help. Yet even two decades later, someone is putting Abby in the cross fire of the Kolton Lake killer. Scott's mission is to solve the case but Abby's quickly becoming his first—and only—priority.

#2209 THE RED RIVER SLAYER

Secure One • by Katie Mettner

When a fourth woman is found dead in a river, security expert Mack Holbock takes on the search for a cunning serial killer. A disabled vet, Mack is consumed by guilt that's left him with no room or desire for love. But while investigating and facing danger with Charlotte—a traumatized victim of sex trafficking—he must protect her and win her trust...without falling for her.

#2210 CRASH LANDING

by Janice Kay Johnson

After surviving a crash landing and the killers gunning for them, Rafe Salazar and EMS paramedic Gwen Allen are on the run together. Hunted across treacherous mountain wilderness, Gwen has no choice but to trust her wounded patient—a DEA agent on a dangerous undercover mission. Vowing to keep each other safe even as desire draws them closer, will they live to fight another day?